An Array of Life

The Nature of an Edmonton Anthology

Edited by

Destanee Charrois
Kat Gawalko
Chelsea Hubbard
Alana Massey

For Amanda,

Thanks for your support!

yours,
Ayster
Lee

Cover art by Isabelle Kuzio
ikuzio@ualberta.ca

Narmer's Palette, Edmonton.

All rights reserved.
ISBN-13:
978-1511442916

ISBN-10:
1511442913

*"Good books, good friends,
and a sleepy conscience:
this is the ideal life."*

– Mark Twain

CONTENTS

Introduction

INTRODUCTION

What started out as an obligatory Edmonton based English project soon blossomed into a thoughtful and cohesive collaboration. It blossomed in such a way that each piece could be related back to an aspect of nature, creating several themes: human nature, Mother Nature, and the cycles of life. Between inspired writers and the fresh enthusiasm of our bright University of Alberta team, we have assembled a humble anthology full of intrigue. Each piece was carefully handpicked, just like any fruit that you would overpay for at an organic grocery store. However, as we're sure you will find, the fruits of our labor are much more cost effective. And who are you kidding, the variety platter at your regular grocer is more than satisfying and provides an array of flavor. So you see, we have tried to provide you with the best of both worlds, taking great care in selecting each piece, as well as providing a collection that will appeal to your every emotion. Enjoy!

SEASONS OF LIFE
SOPHIE LAWSON

The cure for betrayal is
Forgiveness is
Compassion is
Memory is
Life is

Crisp and cold interactions,
An abandonment of comfort
And familiarity.
A dilapidated building,
Unfinished dome
Reaching skyward,
Deserted.
Fur coats of dust
In an artificial and calloused world.
Cranes and scaffolding stand
Idly by,
Abandoned by an escape from
Despair and harshness.
The world comes undone
In a moment,
Unexpected, and continuous.
Hitchhike through an unknown land
Traverse the waves of uncharted territory,
Burying the past, ready
To be uncovered by the upcoming
Arrival of an undisclosed future.
Break free from the imaginary
Prison of life.
Entranced by frivolous
Fictional revelries,
Dreams fail to order perspective,
Unable to refrain
From conceptualized captivity

Of the mind,
Eternal subjectivity,
Locked in a subconscious effort
To undo what is done.

The solution to hopelessness is
Comfort is
Acceptance is
Meaning is
Future is

A static television
Gains clarity
Like a window clearing of frost.
Expectation makes way for reality,
As a child dismisses the concept
Of coloring in the lines.
Rainbows hold secrets of
Habitual repetition,
New and old
The same and all so different.
Promises of authenticity merge with
Fantasy.
Move away into consciousness
Transition from imagination,
To reality.
From reality to imagination.
Darkness follows the implosion
Of self, as boundaries collide.
Ambivalent pages of another's
Biography, bring
A sense of belonging
And not.
The beginnings of escape, from
The prison of self-creation
A patchwork fix to the dome that
Is no-one's home,
Reborn.
Life of varying shapes and sizes,

Yet always the same
Circle.
Biking, riding, cycling
Through the terraces of the innocent
Ones, whose time will surely come.
Meaning is unattainable through life,
Only death.
Always death.

The treatment for loneliness is
Vivid is
Companionship is
Love is
Knowledge is

Inescapable pressure of a
Uniform society
Where each one is
Never the same.
Exposed like a photograph
The flash undiluted by
Human invention.
The world becomes
Sepia,
A wasteland of effort.
A battle of strength,
The loser must fall, hard and fast
Back to the nether space
It emerged from.
Stopped only by a sheer force of will
The flash of existence
Stretched beyond means.
Once caves of wonder,
Now simply
Caves of solitude,
Isolation and trepidation.
Controlled by intense fear,
A fear of not fearing something.

Nothing.
Mathematical equations and
Run on sentences.
Descriptions of a world
Without explanation.
Read between the lines,
Remove layer by layer
Through intensity,
And decipher every code.
Or skip to the last page.
It all ends the same.
Never and always.

The remedy for sadness is
Profound is
Realization is
Understanding is
Happiness is

Knowledge beyond
The limits of experience,
Haggard and dejected.
What once was
Is now no longer.
A game of hangman
With an unknown alphabet.
Cheated, with no hope to win.
Unbroken nostalgia
For what was,
Or perhaps for what was
Never there.
Experiences had,
And regretted alike
Make the most of what is gone
I'm unsure if it will come back.
Multiculturalism spreads its wings
While patriotism falls from on high,
As it is swept aside

On a gust of wind.
The fear is gone.
No more caves of solitude, or
Stripping of layers,
Now comes the remodel.
Replace the once removed,
Harness the memory of
Sweltering despair,
And shore up defenses
Against what is to come.
Since all that once lives,
Must fall in the end.

Rain and childhood,
Long past,
Since gone.
Make way for snow
And the ability for growth.
Snow leads to rain,
But always returns,
Transitions of one to the other
Is subtle, minute,
Expansive and distinct.
A continual loop,
Seemingly unending,
Do not pause, fast forward,
Rewind or repeat.
Simply play.

The purpose of life is
Infinite is
Indeterminate is
Meticulous is
Unknown is

ASCENSION
CHELSEA LUDWIG

I know how this story ends.

He's going to leave me. He'll take to the sky and I'll never see him again. I'll never hear his energetic voice, or feel the chill of his eyes on me, or outline his ear with the pad of my thumb. They say that when the Ascendants transcend this realm, they join everything — the air, the plants, the very fabric of our reality — so they never truly leave us. And that sounds wonderful, it does, but Suki will still be gone.

Just thinking about his Ascension, his final departure, makes my body feel hollow, and an ache like hunger blooms in my chest. It was he who taught me the scope of emotions; how physical they can be, among other things. I wonder if he ever learned anything from me...

Or if he'll remember it when he joins the Stream.

Long after the sun has hidden behind the horizon and the night chill has set in, the traditional Ceremony of One bonfire blazes at the center of a lively throng of villagers. The crackling and hissing of burning blubber underscores the sounds of the festivities; clay cups clink dully, laughter mingles with smoke above our heads, and feet stamp to the sharp tam-tam of rabbit-skin drums. Little ones can be seen ducking among legs, eyes flashing, getting as close as they can to the flame before the heat singes the hairs on their arms and they dart away, screeching in delight.

Everyone's skin is painted. Bright blue, rich purple, and bloody scarlet vegetable dyes are the colors of joy. The colors of celebration.

My face and limbs may be decorated, but I don't feel much like celebrating.

Suki sits close to the fire, on the other side of the circle from me. Our elders, known as the Eyes for the dutiful and revered work they do constantly peering into the Stream, mill around him. I smirk despite my mood. The Ceremony of One is the only time they allow themselves to close their eyes to the Stream and join us here in the now — and they tend to use this miniature holiday to drink entirely too much mead. The last time there was a Ceremony, a couple cycles back, the four of them were found the next morning scattered and dozing all around town, the acrid smells of smoke, sweat, and fermentation steaming from their skin.

Suki is fidgeting and jumpy, but that's normal these days. He's close to Ascension; the Ceremony is always held when the Ascendant feels their time coming — or ending, as I've come to think of it. A pang rings throughout my body. I remember, before he felt the changes, before his impending Ascension began to really take a toll on his mind, when it seemed as though nothing could penetrate his perpetually upbeat demeanor and general goofiness.

In the flickering light of the pyre, I can see his head snap around in different directions. I can imagine his dark eyes snagging on invisible things in the air — no, not invisible; things only he is able to see. My throat closes, and I gulp air and saliva until I can breathe normally again. This is an honor, I remind myself. But it's hard to truly believe when he's the distracted, twitchy shadow of who he used to be. We're told how the Ascendants begin to see the fabric of time and space as they grow closer to their time, but they never tell you how terrible it is to watch the person you love see right through you, or reach for things they can't touch.

I've known Suki since before either of us could even access the Stream, but we weren't at all close back then. We were in the same gen, along with seven other males, and couldn't have been more different. He has an easy way about him, with a smile that jumps quickly onto his lips and a laugh that can't help but infect others. I was born to hunt. I've always been more of an observer, quiet, determined, and athletic; all traits that lend themselves to the quiet escalation of physical excitement whilst waiting, stalking — and then the burst of muscle and sinew and precision of the strike! The onetime Suki came hunting, he fumbled and dropped his spear by simply standing around, and I almost throttled him when his casual conversation caused our prey to scamper out of harm's way.

And now thinking of losing him makes my heart seize. I stare down at the sliver of rabbit jerky between my fingers. I can feel the salt from the meat dusting my fingertips. When did I fall so hard for Suki? It snuck up on me; one day I awoke curled against him, and realized I could think of no other place I would rather be.

I bite into the jerky, trying to enjoy how the meat tears in strips, how the salt lightly burns my tongue. There was an evening after the return of our hunting party. Everyone was sitting around a much smaller fire, chatting idly, and tearing gleefully into the rabbit we had managed to take down. Before the polar shift, rodents were much smaller and could feed maybe two people, but now they're as large as those horses, and are a handsome kill that can feed the village for weeks — if you can avoid their powerful back legs.

I had finished my portion and was picking my way through the huts on my way to relieve myself, when I almost tripped over his outspread legs. My first flash of emotion was annoyance — who sits propped up against a hut all alone, especially when it's meal time? — but then I noticed the tracks that cut through the dirt on his cheeks, leaving salty trails of brown skin. He looked up at me, startled, and rubbed his face furiously.

"What's wrong," I inquired gruffly. I really needed to use the privy, but he was obviously suffering — and if we have learned anything from the Stream and the things it can show us about the past, it's the importance of compassion. Plus, it was just plain odd to see Suki in any kind of distress.

He sighed, holding up a jagged length of bone, a healthy amount of meat still clinging to its porous surface. It was cooked and greasy, and his palm glistened.

"It's just so…fresh," he mumbled. He swallowed, hard, and looked away from his meal. "The Stream is always there, buzzing around, but sometimes it decides to strike out at the silliest things, you know?"

I didn't know, and I told him so.

That's when his eyes, dark, glassy with tears, and confused, met mine. Bodily needs forgotten, I squatted down beside him. We were about the same height and body type — everyone in the village pretty much is — but cycles of hunting had changed my body, and I was bigger. Denser. He was lean, and I felt the difference. "I've never gotten emotions from the Stream," I admitted. "Just images, and only if I choose to dip into it. You…feel things?"

He gulped, muscles in his throat shifting, and nodded. "All the time. Whether I want to or not."

"What about good emotions?" I asked, trying to cheer him up. He shrugged, and sniffed. I mulled over this new experience of the Stream. He was right, it did buzz around just out of consciousness, but I could only zoom into certain situations if I really concentrated—the Eyes said this talent becomes easier with practice, but they'd never said anything about it striking out on its own, or a person being able to get more than images from it. Imagine, being suddenly struck by emotions you couldn't understand or control. "Hmm. I wonder if you'd be able to tap into happy moments, and let them pick up your mood," I mused.

He laughed hoarsely, drawing my attention to his face and, unexpectedly, the fan of his black eyelashes. "I'd never even thought of that." He wiped his eyes once more, and this time when he looked at me, he seemed to take in more than just my appearance. He smiled, and this was the first of many times it made my breath catch. "Thank you, Nuhad."

I grinned, then stood suddenly as my bodily needs surged back to me. "No problem. Gotta go!"

Omree. Suki's voice, soft like the touch of grass, whispers in my head. It cuts through the noises of a village in full festival mode. Omree. Looking across at him, he appears to be completely out of it, but nobody else refers to me as "my life" in a long dead language…also, nobody else can speak to me in thoughts. I wonder if the Eyes know about this phenomenon, about how, after a regular person like me is sexually intimate with an Ascendant, they can share minds. The things he's shown me…

But he's calling me. And now I see why. The Eyes that flanked him protectively have imbibed enough mead to cause them to abandon their casual posts, step out of the ring of villagers and launch into a ballad at the top of their lungs. As the general attention turns to the four very revered, very drunk individuals whose studies impact the very way we live, I fade away, picking my way through the crowd until I'm on the fringes. The air is noticeably colder outside the ring of bodies, but the light wind is refreshing on my skin. The sky is a purpling bruise. I make my way to Suki; even though he's out of sight, I can feel him, as if he's in the periphery of my senses. Another side effect, I suppose.

Finally, I sidle up and sit cross-legged at his side. Wordlessly, he leans into me, and I drape an arm around his shoulder.

"Isn't it beautiful," he says dreamily, voice croaking. He's staring at the fire, and the flames are indeed beautiful, licking the air and waving entrancingly, but I know that isn't what he's talking about.

"What do you see?" I ask quietly. He smiles his crooked smile.

"Threads. Millions and millions of threads, all different, but the same. It's time. But time is…not. And colors…" He breaks off, and sniffs loudly.

"What?" I demand, pulling his fire-warmed body into mine, and inspecting his face, "what's wrong?"

He shakes his head and draws circles on the skin just above my knee with his finger. "It's nothing. It's silly."

"You're always crying," I tease.

When he turns his head and kisses me, I can taste the salt on his lips. I can feel them twist into a smile.

"Are you afraid of dying?"

Suki and I were sitting on the edge of our canyon, kicking our legs over the void. It's a rip in the earth a few hours from our village, and this is where we could be alone together. Not that we couldn't spend time together in the village, but here, we felt free. The air that day was heavy and hot; we expected a storm that night.

"I don't think so," I said carefully. "I like to think about this life."

Suki nodded, thoughtful, and stared up at the aqua sky. Barely discernable wisps of white lazily drifted across our vision, slowly gathering. "Why?"

He swung his legs, swirling a cloud of dirt-dust into being. "Ascending is dying."

I could only stare at him, mouth agape. Before that moment, I had never thought of it that way. Ascending was...it was the next step in our evolution; it was becoming a part of the fabric of reality, becoming a part of the Stream. It was more than just death, it had to be, or...

He was looking at me. "Nuhad?"

I cleared my throat, but could still only croak: "It isn't."

Suki snorted. "How can you be so sure? How can you be sure I won't just blink out of existence? The one thing the Stream can't tell us: what happens when we die." He leaned back onto his elbows, and cocked his head, pondering the blue expanse above us. The ends of his thick brown hair were damp and his brown skin glistened. "It's amazing how, even with this ability to tap into the Stream, into past human consciousness, we're still just guessing. We're making up stories to make ourselves feel better. I mean, another tribe could operate under a completely different set of beliefs, and we'd have no way to tell who's closer to the truth!"

My mouth was dry and I felt like I couldn't get enough air into my lungs. "What you're saying—"

Suki shook his head and laughed, but while his lips curved, his eyes remained overcast. "All through time people have made up stories, and bought into them. Like, like..." He tilted his head and I could see his eyes glaze over; he was searching the Stream. It amazed me how quickly he could dip in and out. "Prophets and gods, heavens and hells." He shook his head, then shifted his weight so he was on his side, facing me. He grinned crookedly. "If those guys are right, we are definitely going to that hell place."

He fell silent then, and wrapped his fingers around my hand, pulling it out of my lap to rest on the dirt between us. Above us, clouds had found company, and the sky was dotted with fluffy white continents.

I'm sorry, omree. I say things sometimes.

I shook my head and tugged my hand out of his grasp. It was easy to forget how effortlessly he could read me, especially when he mostly made a point of staying out of my head.

"If Ascending is dying, then why can't it wait?" I was repeating what he had already heard, but I needed to say it out loud. And then my mind began to explore the possibilities his notion had unlocked. "And does that mean all this leading up to that point is just the descent into madness?" I stared at my hands, but didn't see them. "What's the point? What's even the point of life, then, if we just blink out? What's the point of all the happiness, and the suffering, all the hard work and — "

Suki's body slammed into mine, knocking the air out of my lungs, and he wrestled against me until he was sitting on my hips, my wrists anchored under his ankles. His hands pressed into my shoulders. With my hunter's body, the only chance he ever had of overcoming me was with the element of surprise. When I moved to overpower him, he wiggled his hips, and I laughed, aroused despite myself.

"Enough! Suki." His face was so close to mine, but I refused to let him distract me. "I can't — "

Whatever happens, whatever the point is, or whatever the Stream really is — his eyes bored into mine, fierce and alight — it can't keep me from you.

I rolled my eyes, but felt my doubts ebb. If he believed that even a little bit, and I did too, then maybe it would be enough.

"Now," Suki said aloud, and pecked me lightly on the lips. "Howabout I teach you some more archaic curse words?"

We spent the rest of the day hurling profanities into the canyon.

When the bonfire begins to dwindle, and the cold of night creeps into the bones of even the drunkest Eye, people begin to leave for the warmth of their huts and skins. I touch Suki's elbow, and pull him to his feet. He is so malleable now. I wonder if he would have sat there in the darkness the whole night, staring at whatever it is he sees.

We walk side by side to his hut, not clasping fingers, but at all times touching: shoulder to shoulder, hip to hip, straying hands. When we reach his hut, I pause, then lean in to kiss him goodnight out of habit. His lips move against mine.

"Stay with me tonight," he says, voice husky. "Please."

We do not have sex that night. While I would welcome the distraction, I feel like his atoms will split apart if I'm not careful. I wrap my arms around him, though, pressing our bodies together until I can feel his heart flutter against my chest.

21

"I'm not scared," he mutters into my neck, voice scraping in his throat. I tighten my grip; maybe if I hold him hard enough, he won't go.

"Me neither," I croak, and feel him snort. "I'm still hungry, that's why I'm shaking."

He snuggles into my neck, and his lips tingle at my collarbone. "You're always hungry."

In that moment, I can almost forget what's coming. It could almost be any other night: back at his hut after a village celebration, too tired to have sex but awake enough to exchange drowsy words, limbs winding around limbs, until we both doze off.

In the morning, when I'm awoken by sunlight breaking through slits in the hut's walls, my arms are empty.

MY DADDY'S EYES
AUSTEN LEE

"Just walk in there like you own the place," Dad says to me. He is kneeling down, talking to me so close that I can almost feel the rough tickle of his goatee on my face.

He is smiling. His teeth are long and remind me of piano keys, despite the fact that they are stained yellow from drinking too much coffee and smoking too many cigarette butts—old piano keys. As I look over him, I wonder if my teeth have turned brown from drinking so much chocolate milk. I always have chocolate milk while Dad drinks his coffee.

We have just come from the diner, where the walls are pale yellow and my feet dangle far from the floor because the stools are so tall. Dad was reading the newspaper. His fingers stroked the edge of the pages rhythmically, turning black from the ink rubbing onto his skin.

"Do you know what day it is?" He asked me.

"No," I said, "what day?"

He smiled, a sad kind of smile, and said, "It's Mommy's day."

I knew what that meant. So far there have been two Mommy's days, where we visit her, say hello and tell her that I'm doing well in school. Even though that's a lie. I don't go to school anymore. I bet Mommy knows we are lying, but I don't say anything to Daddy about it. He says that she can hear us, even from all the way down there: deep, deep in the snow.

I can't really remember what I look like anymore. I haven't seen a proper mirror in a long time. Sometimes I make faces in the backs of the spoons at the diner. I know that the way I appear in them is just a trick, but I worry my face has actually become that way. All I know is that Daddy tells me I am pretty. I trust him, but I can't be completely sure because of the reflection in the spoons.

It's just the two of us now; we eat at diners and sleep where we can find. Daddy drinks coffee and I drink chocolate milk. The coffee is the only thing that has stayed the same, since Daddy got sad and stopped going to work.

"We have to get Mommy a present." Dad told me at the diner.

"What kind of present?" I asked.

Dad picked up his coffee cup; his fingernails black underneath. I watched his throat as he threw his head back and drank the rest of his coffee. The bulb that protrudes from his neck slid up and down as he swallowed.

I'm looking at that bulb now, as we stand in a cold, slush-covered parking lot.

"I'm scared." I tell him, and as I speak a small cloud of white appears before me. It hovers for a moment in the cold air. I think that I look like Dad when he smokes, but I do not have a cigarette butt.

"You're a warrior," Dad says. He lifts a hand and rubs his thumb across both of my cheeks. I can feel him paint two lines of dirt and grime on the surface of my skin. "It won't take long." He says, "Do you remember what to do?"

"Yes." I say.

"Tell me."

"Get the red ones." I answer.

"And?" Dad says.

"Walk in like I own the place."

"Good girl."

Dad pats me on the head with his big, rough hand. It is nearly the size of my face and it makes me feel small when it is clamped onto my skull. I shake him off and ask, "What did you draw on me?"

There is silence for a moment. My father's face becomes serious, his musical piano key smile fading away behind his lips. I know he is going to tell me something important.

"I drew marks on your cheeks," Dad tells me, "to cast a spell on you."

"What kind of spell?" I say, the skin beneath my eyes suddenly feeling alive, prickling with the gentle pulsation of magic. Or could it be frostbite?

"It makes you invisible." He says.

"Forever?"

"No, not forever." Dad explains, "Only for a little while, so you have to be fast."

"How fast?"

"It's already wearing off."

Dad is looking at me straight in the eyes. His pupils are small, contracting against the brightness shining off the snow in the parking lot. As I stare back at him, I am thinking about colouring a picture of the ocean. The crayon I am using is the perfect shade of blue, full sized, not broken from squeezing too tight or being dropped on the floor. I imagine stroking it across the page, staying inside all the lines without fail.

In my mind, I show my mother the finished drawing, envision her smile; she is so amazed. I tell her that the ocean is my Daddy's eyes, just like his smile is piano keys, and she takes the paper in her hands. She says that it is "fridge material". That was what she always said whenever I made something really good.

"Hurry now."

Dad's face disappears as he spins me around. I see the grey exterior of the building I am about to enter. People are passing by with loud, rattling, metal grocery carts. They're fighting to push them against the density of the brown slush that has gathered in front of the store. I take a step forward, being careful not to let it splash up onto my tights.

The sliding glass doors that lead into the supermarket swallow me with one swift gulp. Now I am tall enough to set off the motion sensor. When I was smaller I would have to wait for someone else to walk up to the door and then run in behind them.

I feel grown up as I enter the cold, tiled store, forgetting the smallness that had just previously overcome me beneath the grip of my father's giant hand on my scalp. A sense of bravery fills my chest, and for an instant I wish that I wasn't invisible, because I want everyone to see what a big girl I am.

My cheeks burn. I scan the store quickly for the colour red. Everything is taller than me; I crane my neck and catch flashes of orange, indigo, green. These are the designs on packages, the skins of fruits, and the patterned skirt of a woman browsing a few steps away from me. I can see every shape and shade except for red, silky red, sweet smelling like chocolate and perfume.

I can feel myself crumbling. My heart pounds inside my ears, tha-rump, tha-rump, tha-rump, and I can't help but wonder why

I had to walk in like I owned the place if nobody was going to see me.

One last, quick scan, I decide. I've only been roaming around for about a minute, but it feels like I have been trapped inside the chilled, sour-smelling room for hours. If I can't find what I'm looking for, I'm leaving. Dad will be disappointed.

I stop dead. There they are! I've found them, red as blood and finger-paint. I scamper across the store, arms outstretched, and clamp onto the thorny stems. Ouch, but I don't pause. I still own the place; my cheeks are hot. The woman in the patterned skirt is looking at me. I can feel her gaze, but pretend that I don't see her. I try to make myself believe that there really is magic rippling all over my skin.

I leave the store and Dad is standing right where I left him, smoking a cigarette. I can tell that it's a full sized one. He must have "bummed" it off someone else this time, rather than smoking one he'd found on the ground.

I run toward him, but he doesn't see me. He is looking out toward the street, white acrid smoke erupting from his lips. Sweat leaks out of my pores, and the magic paint drawn along my cheeks begins to melt. Slushy water is spraying up everywhere from beneath my feet. I no longer care about my tights.

Suddenly I'm flying. I feel myself soaring through the air. I can tell my ankle is twisted, having been caught on a clump of packed mud and snow.

A splash of red slips out of my hands, petals and stems twist and contort, quickly dying in the frost. I strike the concrete with a force strong enough to knock the breath out of my lungs. A noise squeals out of me like air coming out of a tire. I see the roses spread out in the snow.

Dad turns in my direction, and sees my body looking like a pile of clothes and hair. I'm trying to get up so that he knows I am OK. I wonder, am I still invisible?

I hear Dad's voice, "Baby!"

I can see him running across the parking lot, cigarette still between his teeth, leaving embers behind him. I want to ask, "Can you see me?" But I cannot catch my breath.

He must see me though, because he is running in my direction. Then finally I am being lifted into his arms. My breath returns to me, and I inhale small gulps of air past the fabric of Dad's shirt. I press my face into him. I can smell him. He smells like the beach in the morning; damp air, filled with the smell with coffee and tobacco and salt. I taste salt, too. Or am I crying?

Dad is whispering into my ear, "Good job, honey. You did so good."

He is petting my hair.

"She's so proud of you." He tells me, "You've made her so happy."

My lungs hurt too much to talk.

I am still in his arms. Then I feel us kneel down together as he gathers up the roses from the ground with the hand that is not holding me. Over his shoulder I can see that he has left some petals behind. They are stuck in the snow, half buried in the murky white slush. The fresh mud around it, turned up from Dad's feet, almost resembles the colour of chocolate milk.

I close my eyes and inhale again, nuzzling my face into Dad's fuzzy neck. He smells like sweat — the beach in the morning. But I never have been to the ocean.

DUST MOTES
TAYLOR WITIW

Swooshing air and loud, monotonous beeping burst into the bus as Anne Garvie cracked a passenger window. The breeze felt warm, but she hoped it would still be able to cool the torrid plastic of her seat. Anne tilted her head into the aisle to see through the windshield at the front of the bus. Ahead, the traffic circle was down to one lane and the driver, seeing a small window of opportunity, took to the circle much quicker than he ought to have. As the heavy vehicle wheeled about, the force of the turn pressed Anne toward the window. The sensitive skin of her upper arm slid and touched the rim of her seat, which had not yet cooled. "Ouch!" she cried; her face went hot red with embarrassment. Anne turned to the window again to hide from the other passengers. Glimpsing the Idylwylde library, she half stood and pulled the long yellow cord with her smarting arm, while rubbing it vigorously with the other. She sat back down with an ungracious thump and looked about, head lowered. A few of the other passengers were looking at her. Evidently, they had noticed her little outburst. Feeling a fresh wave of blush creep across her cheeks, she kept her gaze low and sat fidgeting until the bus came to a stop.

Standing with her face toward a blue bus shelter, Anne brushed her skirt. Another bus approached. She held her knee-length, flower-patterned skirt down while it passed with a refreshing tumult. Almost in synchrony, the heavens offered their own clamour. Smiling, Anne looked up to the quickly clouding sky and then back to the traffic circle. The orange vested workers beyond the reflector capped pylons were also looking up. From their direction, the smell of fresh asphalt wafted toward her. Turning away from the circle, Anne started home, taking long strides with her slender legs. Across the street and behind a chain link fence, other youth ran a red gravel circuit or lounged on the grass circle in the centre. Anne was happy to be going home for lunch. Father was going to be there. She looked to the right and was pleased to see how quickly she could make the dark spruce tree, pair of budding leafed trees, small square hedge, and light post pass. She imagined how quickly she could make them fly by if she had a bike. It would probably be like riding the bus, only she wouldn't have to worry about a scorching seat. As she thought, a passing car came too near the curb, flinging dust into her eyes.

Anne stopped. She squeezed her eyes shut and rubbed them with her knuckles. Then blinking, she waited to start walking again until her eyes reoriented after being squished so eagerly. Coming back into focus, they adjusted to the image of her small, knotted fists. She didn't really like the deep-set liver spots that came into view, but she extended her fingers and they were still slim and beautiful. Picking up her pace again, she saw the school's empty soccer field on the left and the Bonnie Doon Mall on the right. She looked back at her finger nails. *Maybe it's time to do something about these. There's that salon in the mall Helen mentioned at fancy tea.* Anne stared at the concrete monstrosity, but kept walking home. Some vague, half-forgotten responsibility prevented her from making the detour. The dry, prairie heat began to irritate her throat. She reached into her purse and retrieved a bottle of water. The pure, cool liquid was almost sweet. Mother had always insisted she not leave home without a thermos of water.

Rain drops darkened the ground near her worn running shoes. Anne thought her thermos of water funny, since the sky was about to give her more than she needed. She added a bit of a skip to her brisk pace but the sky gods, determined not to let her escape, emptied their thermoses on her. Purse swinging and shoes flopping, she ran laughing down the sidewalk. The wet and cold were only temporary, only for this moment. Soon she would be home, with a cup of warm heather tea and a steaming plate of shepherd's pie. Rumbling from the clouds above, the sky gods cursed their ineffectiveness. At the last bus shelter before eighty second avenue, Anne stopped to grab a paper for Father from one of the newsstand boxes. She pulled her long, now sopping, blonde hair away from her eyes and dropped a coin in. She reached for the handle.

The hot metal burnt her hand. Worse yet, she realized there was not a single paper in the box. *How did I not notice? I could have sworn I checked the little window. We're going to have to call you absent-minded Annie.* She giggled a little, but it turned to a heavy sigh. Now her hand and her arm were sore. She stood up straight, shielding her eyes from the glare off the windshields of passing cars. Propelled by she knew not what, Anne began jogging, albeit a bit sullenly, toward the stoplights. Home. She just wanted to get home, but the solid orange hand said no, not yet. The sun was clearly thinking about setting, but refused to let off the heat. As she waited in limbo, she looked down eighty-second street and saw the spinning mall sign cast unusual reflections. It was, to her, like a windmill of light.

The sky was dark, the rain heavy, and the light turned green. Anne's joy regrouped and a fierce smile asserted itself on her face. She ran across the street, then into and through the geometric, residential maze like a mad woman. She was alone. No onlookers beheld her; no neighbors peered from behind their curtains. Anne reached for the rain in ecstasy, opening and squeezing her hands shut, trying to catch the rain, but in a way that was not really trying. She knew why Mother had told her to come home for lunch. Father had been saving up. He had bought a bicycle for her Birthday. A beautiful white one with a basket on the front, the one she had cut out of the sears catalogue but "lost". She ran faster. He would take her to the shed when she got home, out into the rain. Mother would watch from the window.

She knew. She knew and the weight of it hit her. Anne stopped before her house. The rain quit. She knew the end to this story; it had passed years ago. She stared at her dishevelled, generational house and, between blinking tears away, saw it both as it had been, with fresh paint on all the trim and a lawn cut like a military man's head, and as it was. Anne brushed aside the wiry grey strands that imprisoned her sight. She saw the door opening and began walking toward it, knowing she would have to open it herself.

As she walked up her crumbling concrete patio stone path, the juniper, which had seemed such a good idea years ago, reached out with unruly, burnt-red arms to rasp her soft ankles. Its spiny, segmented leaves broke off like miniature caltrops, attaching themselves to her shoes, skin, and the fringe of her skirt. She did not know if it was dead. She did not care. With long strides, she ascended three concrete stairs, her hand brushing the bubbling paint of the iron railing. She fumbled with her keys before opening the door.

Musk tumbled out of her house and into the aging street. Leaving her purse on the antique drink table by the front door, she reached for the golfer-headed shoe horn. In the struggle to remove her shoes while accommodating a sore back, Anne's gaze lifted to a photograph resting on the half-wall to her left. There, in front of the wooden, ornamental posts stretching to the ceiling, a man, two young girls, and the young woman, who she knew as herself, smiled back. Kicking off a reluctant shoe, Anne stepped forward, her eyes fixed on the man in the scene. She frowned. Lost to time, she stood still, hardly blinking. *Ted.* A weary smile appeared on her face as she reached to touch his, but the glass surface of the photo could not satisfy what she was reaching for. Anne picked up the photo and walked past the living room into the kitchen. She set the picture down on the kitchen table by her Aricept and some wilted wild flowers, which, ironically, were in a painted vase depicting bright, colourful ones.

Stepping past the table, Anne found the string for the wooden blind. She tugged at it and the kitchen filled with tangerine light. She stood by the window for a moment, but found she could not bear the sight of the rusted tin shed in the back, where an ancient white bicycle sat. She returned to the table and sat. Dust motes swirled about her like memories, glimmering in the dusk light.

THE BEAUTY OF MAGIC
SCOTT MEEBERG

> *"I guess I could be pretty pissed off about what*
> *happened to me... but it's hard to stay mad, when*
> *there's so much beauty in the world."*

> – Lester Burnham
> *American Beauty*

In a meadow far away, a small boy awoke from his sleep and looked around. His thoughts danced through his mind, scattered and broken. He strained to hold them still, trying his hardest to grasp even a single word to describe what he was seeing. *Beauty.* Finally, a word burst through the chaos, pouring from his mind and painting the sun-kissed meadow with bold strokes. Words appeared in its wake, naming the sights. *Tree. Grass. Butterfly. Flower. Sun. Bright. Warm. Open. Empty. Alone.* The last word interrupted his reverie, as he realized that he was truly and completely alone. Despite the warmth and brightness of it all, the meadow was utterly silent. There was no wind whispering across the grass. The birds far, far above sang no song, and if not for the butterflies and birds flitting about his meadow, he could have been in a painting.

He thought he had never been more alone in his life, but he had no way of being certain, for his memories seemed locked behind a massive wall in his mind, with only a trickle of words to explain where he was. Some of them made sense to him, and he placed them around the meadow where they belonged. *White.* That was the colour of the...*Clothes* covering his body. *Bark.* That was on the tree beside him. *Yellow.* That was the grass, now slowly swaying in the still silent wind. *Run.* He began to move now, churning his legs back and forth, speeding faster and faster across the field. After what seemed like only a moment, he turned back and was...*Surprised* at how far he'd gone. The tree was now just a speck in the distance, but the meadow stretched on, endless and beautiful. *Blue.* That was the sky above him, and as he looked up at the infinite blueness, he couldn't help but feel that something wasn't right. Something was missing. The wall in his mind pulsed, and the meadow pulsed with it. There was a life to the air, just for a second, and as the pulse faded, there was a stream of words, all of them as meaningless and empty as the now-still air. *Paper. Tile. Dog. Fire. Heavy. Fairy. Water. Pass. Wash. Mother.* No, no, that one was something. There was a place for that one...what is it? He struggled for a moment, but finally let the word slip away, quickly forgetting it as he noticed the sky was now dotted with...*Clouds.*

It was beautiful. Everything was so, so beautiful. The boy ran through his meadow, stopping to dance with a butterfly before it flew off to ballet alone over the flowers, stopping to smell each flower, letting their scents kiss his nose before spinning around, finally collapsing from the sheer beauty of it all. Words came together in his mind, something he had heard before, but he couldn't picture when or where. *"There's so much beauty in the world, I feel like I can't take it, and my heart is just going to cave in."* He wasn't what all that meant, but he knew that it was exactly how he felt, his heart racing to keep up with everything his senses were taking in. As he stood still to feel the beat of his heart in his chest, he realized that the air was pulsing along with his heart, like the meadow and everything in it was one giant living thing, and he was in tune with it all. Though there was still not a sound to be heard, the beauty before him was like music, and he felt that if he could just do it right, he could be the conductor of everything around him.

Far, far away, and yet very, very close, a mother cried.

The boy's attempts to bend the meadow to his imagined song were interrupted by a burst of...*Rain* from the sky, and suddenly more words became clear in his mind. *Water.* That was what was falling from the clouds above. *Wet.* That was what he was becoming, his thin clothes pressing against his skin. *Wash.* That was what the rain was doing to him, washing his body clean of what little...*Dirt* he had picked up in his playing. His mind as well, all thoughts of the living field now draining with the rain into the soil beneath his bare feet. Words weren't so focused now; he just knew what things were. The wall in his mind was cracked, and his thoughts flowed faster by the minute. If only there was some way to break that wall down. He closed his eyes, trying to enter his mind, to really see the barrier. After what seemed like hours of staring intensely into the blackness of his closed eyelids, he began to feel a sucking inside of him, as if someone had a straw in his brain and was trying to drink the rest of him through it like a meaty milkshake. He allowed the sucking to continue, and finally, slowly, light began to creep in. Blurry at first, it gradually became clearer and clearer, until he could tell exactly what he was looking at.

He was inside his mind, the sky darkened by a covering of deep green clouds tinged with blackness. He could see the blockage as well. It was indeed a wall, higher and longer than he could see, blocking off most of the landscape of his mind. It was made up of thousands upon thousands of bricks, and each dark reddish brick had a word or picture on it. Across the stretch of the wall, he could see holes where bricks had come loose, and as he watched, a few more detached themselves and sped away into the green storm above. The wall pulsed slowly, rhythmically, with tiny crackles of electricity appearing for the briefest of instants before vanishing. Now more than ever, this wall seemed alive.

As he focused, he realized that each brick was a memory. He ran to the nearest hole and pried the first brick he saw off of the wall. As he turned the brick over in his hands, he read the word scratched onto its surface. *Apple*. He could taste an apple, smell an apple, see apples. Apple pie, apple cider, apple juice. Green apples, red, Granny Smith, Macintosh, Red Delicious…his thoughts were flooded with memories of every apple he had ever seen, eaten or heard about. It was too much. He threw the brick away, and it rolled against the ground, breaking into pieces as it did. Each bounce and break sent spikes of pain into his head, bringing him to his knees. As quickly as the apple thoughts had entered his brain, they vanished, leaving him unsure what the word he had just learned even was. He couldn't remember it. Looking at this wall, there was so, so much he couldn't remember. He must be very old, to have this many memories.

He leaned his forehead against the wall, tears welling in his eyes. It wasn't fair. There was so much he could see, his whole life being played out in thousands of fragments, each brick a piece of the puzzle. Questions filled his mind: Who was he? Why had this happened to him? What was his name? What was his name? *What was his name?* He pounded his small fists against the bricks, but soon had to stop, as each pound on the wall was a punch to the head. He turned his back to the wall and began to cry. Slowly, he lost concentration, and everything around him melted away, leaving just a scared boy crying in a beautiful, empty field.

King Oulas watched the sun set in the west, as he did every evening. Not a real sun, of course, but the best that the elves who had first traveled here could create with magic, and far more beautiful than the real sun. It was capable of producing light and colours that a human mind would not have been able to comprehend, had any human ever set foot in Tariene. Long ago, the elves had built Tariene as an elven sanctuary, a massive city filled with magic and beauty. As the humans grew more and more violent and jealous of their elven cousins, elves had flocked underground, until none lived on the surface. Humans had long since forgotten elves, remembering them only in myths and legends holding the barest fragments of truth. No living elf remembered life above ground either, no matter what stories some of the elders might tell. Truth be told, few elves had any desire to see the earth's surface. Tariene was so much more beautiful, and elves thrived off of beauty. No magic could occur without beauty, the two were so closely intertwined. With the sun now set, and the magical, artificial moon rising in the sky, Oulas turned to his palace door. The memory of the sun's beauty still in his mind, he opened the door from a distance with a sweeping gesture. As he walked through the door, he made sure it took him into the bedroom where his wife sat, as she always did, in her rigid chair beside the bed.

As he laid eyes on his wife, his heart raced, filling him with a stream of magic so powerful it couldn't be contained. He lit the fireplace, and as the flames roared, he gestured quickly, with almost imperceptible movements, at various carvings, paintings and tapestries around the room, which rearranged themselves to whatever he pleased that night. Many became portraits of Mareina, depicting her from their first meeting to three hundred years later, when they were finally married. A long time, even by elf standards, but they had denying feelings in service of duty for many, many years. Oulas had always found her to be the most beautiful thing in all Tariene. The people said he was the most powerful elf in the land, but his power doubled when his wife was near.

Mareina had been a beautiful young scholar when they had first met, studying magic and trying to push the limits of what could be accomplished by elves. Her magic was wild and chaotic, with the potential to fail at any moment. She constantly had to practice restraint in order to remain calm and controlled, as her power always skirted the edge of causing massive destruction. Oulas found it fascinating how much an elf's magic reflected their personality. His powers were strong but subtle, and very rarely dangerous. Likewise, Oulas prided himself on his ability to keep his temper without fail, and he worked most effectively as a leader by making small reforms, keeping the peace here and there when disputes arose, but ultimately allowing the elves he ruled over to embrace community on their own. He only stepped in when necessary, but when he set his mind to do something, one would be a fool to bet on its failure.

His wife was very much the opposite: brash, strong-willed and opinionated. She could burst into anger in moments and then be smiling and joyous seconds later. She took charge often and was adamant that hers was the only way. They were an unlikely pair, but somehow they had always been perfect together, and everyone could see it. In fact, they had been the last to acknowledge their connection, devoting themselves solely to the service of the realm for 350 years before they gave up resisting the attraction and were married. In retrospect, Oulas regretted waiting so long. Because they were both over 500 years old when they were finally married, they had only been able to have one child, a son named Marquel.

Marquel had always been an odd child, somber and downcast, unable to see the beauty of the world. Oulas had often had to calm Mareina as she panicked for their son's future, worrying that Marquel was "too human," that he had inherited something from her grandfather Nyclas Flamelle, who was rumored to have lived above ground for many years. Regardless of where the boy's abnormal behaviour had come from, the consequences were extremely unusual: whereas most elves had at least some magical ability even from birth, Marquel was unable to do magic of any kind.

The boy's tears finally slowed to a halt, and he lay on the ground drawing ragged breaths. His mind was a fortress, and he had to unlock its vaults and regain who he was. Perhaps a clue was hidden somewhere in the vastness of this meadow. Once again, he tried to concentrate, this time with his eyes open, trying to see every leaf, every blade of grass, trying to search for something that stood out. After a long time of just staring intensely at everything and nothing, he had to admit defeat. The field may be beautiful, but it was empty. He relaxed, lying down on the grass and trying to calm his breathing. He lazily stared into the clear blue sky, dotted with only faint wisps of clouds, and tried to think. Thinking without memory was extremely difficult, and his mind often wandered, focussing on one beautiful view after another. Slowly, he released any conscious control of his thoughts and allowed them to roam free. As he observed the beauty around him, his view began to grow clearer and clearer. He hadn't even realized that he had been viewing the world through a haze, but now that the fog was clearing, he couldn't fathom how he had not known before. The world was so beautiful. He was overcome with a vast sense of joy and knowledge, and he could feel the wall in his mind crumbling faster and faster.

Of course, Oulas and Mareina had tried any way they could think of to induce Marquel into seeing the beauty and the magic of the world, teaching him every technique they had learned in their many years of experience. They had even tried pouring their own magic into him, but magic was challenging enough to use on living organisms, and it seemed to have no effect on Marquel. Despite their worries and fears, they still loved their son with every fiber of their being. That was why the past four months had been so torturous; why Mareina had not left her son's room save for a few minutes at a time, and only when absolutely necessary. On the morning of his 50th birthday, Marquel had been found unconscious on the same balcony where Oulas watched the sun set every night. He had not woken since, even with both his parents and all the most powerful elves in Tariene doing their best to revive and heal him. Elves rarely needed medical care as most wounds could be healed through magic, so there were few who knew anything of healing. No one could determine the cause of Marquel's condition, only that it appeared magical in origin.

The boy could see everything now, down to the smallest molecules in each pebble on the ground. The air, the grass, the trees, everything was brimming with energy, an energy he could feel throughout his body. He stretched out his hands and began to manipulate the molecules he could see, slowly at first, then faster, becoming a potter whose clay was the very world around him. Marquel – for that was his name, he now remembered, his memories returning to him in a massive rush – whirled around, making everything he could see into his plaything. For those moments, he was powerful beyond belief. *So this is what magic feels like*, he realized. He was able to see beyond his meadow now, out of his mind and into Tariene, standing on one of the palace balconies, until he rose even higher and further as the magic within him saw the beauty of the whole earth, as he took in all of human and elf knowledge at once, all of the past, present and future, everything that was, had been, and would ever be. A tsunami of emotion crashed over him, as he wept and laughed and became enraged within the span of mere seconds.

Then suddenly, he lost control.

The reigns of magic that he had held so tightly now slipped from his fingers, and for an instant, he saw a future with everything burning, saw himself alone, the last living creature on a barren planet. He grabbed desperately at the air before him, trying to reign in the catastrophe. It was no use. For a long moment, he despaired, until an idea came to him. Because he had released this horror, perhaps he could contain it?

He steeled himself, preparing for what he would have to do. Then, with a massive press of will, he pulled the strings of magic, drew them back inside himself. The future returned to its natural course, but he could feel that the power bubbling inside him would not be contained for long. In desperation, he sealed it into his mind, locking it behind a wall so vast and large it could never be destroyed. However, this wall was not without cost. To lock away his magic like that required locking away most of himself with it. It was like a drain inside of him, sucking away his memories, sucking away the knowledge he had only just acquired. He wondered what would happen to him. He hoped it would be peaceful, like a nap in a warm summer meadow.

As the king and queen watched, Marquel's eyelids flickered for a few moments, then he stilled once more. Every day for four months, it had been the same. His eyelids would flutter for just a few moments in the evening, then there would be no movement until the same time the next day, exactly 24 hours later.

Oulas remembered the hopes he had had when his son was born. The whole of Tariene had rejoiced with their rulers. Rumors and whispers in the streets all said the same thing: "With parents like that, that boy is going to be the most powerful elf of all time." How sad that the rumors would never come to pass.

BLOOD FLOES

KAYLEIGH CLINE

This hemorrhage
she is washing off her gloves and scrubs
swirls down the steely disinterest of the drain
towards the unreachable zero of gravity...

...and while she rolls hand over hand,
she hones her wayward thoughts
into a force that punches through
the instrument-encrusted walls
of the theatre to the outside,
to where the drain leads:
the river, blooming with ice
that is globular, cellular,
fractal, precise.

This process of washing away
possesses the predictability of poetry,
for this blood is, like the river,
stuck in a half-frozen state
of Novemberness:
equal parts solid and liquid,
enslaved by the throes
of indecisive adolescence,
unable to achieve the assured,
crystalline maturity of ice
in unblemished line.
The liquid plasma is gone
without a backward dance,
but the deep red clots drag
with the elusiveness of ice floes,
resisting the choice between states.

The property of flow forces
rivers and blood to be fleeting
with their hybridity. Meanwhile,

altogether elsewhere,
her photograph is standing
on the back of his black baby grand.

And it fades in the radiation splashed
onto its surface by both the winter sun
and his burning blue eyes.
The captured colors of her
vulnerable to the murderous impulses
of time. The brown of her skin,
the shine of her eyes, even
the heartbreaking red of her sundress —
all of it ebbing into outline and splotch:
solidity of shape swept
away into the flow of light.

And so while she thinks
about rivers and blood
and that false equation
to which we all pray
(movement = life),
these photographic remains of her
are paling like her bled-out patient:
picture-framed by gurney edges,
awaiting a last maturation into meat.

MUFFINS, MUSTARD, BREAD AND PIE

JIM SELLERS

Andy opened his eyes and sat up in a haze of semi-consciousness. He groaned, lowered his stiff legs from the bed to the floor and rubbed his eyes. At 75, his body was slower than his mind at getting back to the land of the living. He turned to look at the clock and smacked his forehead. What was he thinking? It was 9:45 and the store closed at 10:00. He promised his wife he would pick up the groceries for the morning. He jumped off the bed. Silly old goat, he thought to himself, he'd fallen asleep and damn near disappointed her again. He tossed through the bed covers for his clothes. No time to clean up, he had to run. Sweat pants and a t-shirt would have to do. That's all anyone wore these days anyway.

Andy limped down to the hallway closet and dug around for his hat and pulled on a jacket. He padded the pockets for his wallet and started digging around for his car keys. Where the hell were his keys? Did Edith put them away again? He glanced up at the clock on the wall. The store closed in ten minutes. He'd have to walk; there was no time to look for things. He growled and slammed the door behind him. He would have to talk to her about this. Except he already knew what she would say. "You should exercise more, you're not so young." She would taunt him, "you silly old man, why don't you do something with all that spare time? Go out for a walk." It seemed like most of their conversations took the form of criticism and arguments, but they had fallen into a familiarity that came with fifty years of marriage. Andy loved Edith, and she loved him, but that no longer needed to be said. It was the other stuff, the anger and cajoling that helped keep each of them going. Steam engines didn't run on cold water.

Andy stepped out into the evening air. It was fresh and cooler than inside the house. He paused briefly and sucked in as much air as his limited lung capacity could hold. Damn cigarettes; he knew he should have quit long before he did. The walk felt good and the air was helping to clear his head. His naps always made him feel groggy and it took a strong coffee or a shower to clear the crust. Edith told him to stop napping in the afternoon because it ruined his sleep at night and he was always up until the early morning hours, thumping around the house and keeping her awake. Andy chuckled at that. She was always a light sleeper and the slightest sound, like the baby cough or a door creak, would have her up like a guard dog, shielding the family from danger. He had taken to watching TV with the closed captioning so not to wake her. Andy could nap anywhere, anytime but he could only sleep with his wife. Her scent, her shape, her warmth comforted him and took away his anxiety.

Andy lurched down the street, his bad hip complaining as he swayed side to side to keep moving. He had worn his old shoes that were convenient and easy to slip into but they were no good for his feet. The store was less than a block away but he had precious few minutes to get in the door before they could lock him out and send him back to face his wife with another failure on his score card. Every effort to move faster only increased the pain in his legs. Goddamn old age, he muttered. It's nature's evil joke.

Even at that late hour, the noise of the traffic was irritating. The street had been widened to four lanes and traffic lights were put in, which cause a regular roar of engines as they sped off on the green light every few minutes. Things were sure different that when they had first moved to the area. Andy remembered with absolute clarity the day they took possession of their new house. It was 1956 and theirs was one of a few lookalike bungalows in the city's newest subdivision. A single paved road connected them to the outside world. The place was a lone oasis surrounded by mud fields and a beehive of machinery digging out new lots that would eventually become hundreds of new homes with families walking to school, playing in the fields and driving to work.

Edith was the master homemaker. Her home was her castle; contrary to everything Andy had been told about the man being in charge. Edith was the boss and she loved Andy for all of his flaws. He always tried so hard to please her and felt bad every time he disappointed her. She would say nothing but the message on her face was clear. That thought made Andy step up his pace as he crossed the parking lot. Sure enough the stock boy was standing by the door, keys in hand ready to lock up as Andy pulled the door open and stepped in. He smiled triumphantly at the kid, recognizing him immediately as the Johnson boy from down the street. He was the kid that would cut his lawn and shovel the walks. He was a great kid, Andy thought, and now he's working a real job. Boy these kids grow up so fast. Next thing you know, this one will be in college.

"Hey Billy, "Andy greeted the boy. Billy winced at the old man's breath, forcing a smile while turning his head.

"Hi, Mr. Watson, how are you?" the question seemed earnest.

"Never better Billy. I had to run to beat you to the door, eh?" Andy chuckled. The boy looked confused. "I mean, I almost didn't make it." He headed into the store.

"But, I thought you were sick," Billy said.

Andy stopped and turned back to face the boy, "Where the hell did you hear that? I'm a bit slow with the arthritis but still strong where it matters. Know what I mean?" he grinned.

There was an awkward pause, then Andy laughed, pointing to his head. "Up here boy, I know what you were thinking. Ha ha." Andy wondered into the store still chuckling while Billy stepped outside to breathe. He wiped his eyes and pulled out his keys to lock the door.

Andy mumbled his list repeatedly to himself, glancing down the aisles while saying the words: Muffins, mustard, bread and pie. He was disoriented; they must have remodeled the store because nothing was where he remembered it. But, when had they done that, he wondered. Truth be told, he hadn't done much of the shopping. Edith did all the housekeeping jobs while Andy worked. It was the tradition backs then and something they had maintained long after he retired. Andy was happy to respect his wife's space and let her run things around the house. That was her domain; he just lived in it and enjoyed the benefits. Andy chuckled, the lioness runs the den.

All Edith wanted when they were married was a home and a family. She was no career girl; motherhood was her ambition. Andy was prepared to do anything for her, such was the depth of his devotion.

"Promise me we'll have lots of kids, Andy," she said, looking around at the wood floors and the white walls, the new Kenmore appliances and the back yard. Andy promised her, he was willing to raise a dozen kids but Brian, their son, turned out to be an only child. Andy just didn't have any more in him. They tried repeatedly and even considered adoption but, in the end, no more children were to live in their little nest.

Andy spied his neighbors, Frank and Carol Griffin, shopping for vegetables. They were the first people Andy and Edith met on his block when they moved into the house fifty years ago. The Griffins were still Andy's closest friends, literally only steps away down the block. They shared in all their life events together, brought in numerous New Years and celebrated promotions and many summer barbeques. They were practically twin families right up until Edith gave birth to their son. The Griffins never had children, they never said why. Andy hadn't realized until several years had passed just how much they had drifted apart from the Griffins. Having a child and working to pay for a house, a car and the new Motorola TV that dominated their living room had distracted Andy to the point that he rarely spoke to his friends at all. The relationship had been reduced to casual greetings on chance encounters. Andy couldn't remember the last time they talked about anything. He paused and sighed. Time is cold, rushing you on and then reminding you what you missed when it's too late. Standing and watching his old friends shop, Andy felt miles away. He walked down the aisle, reached over and softly tapped Frank on the shoulder. Frank started, grunted and turned around with a scowl.

"Hi ya, Frank, Carol. Long time no see," Andy's voice was clear and cheerful. He smiled with all the warmth he could muster. When their eyes met, Frank's face went white while Carol gasped and clung to her husband's arm. Frank recovered and his scowl returned.

"Andy! Jesus, You scared the everlovin' hell out of me. Good god, you know my wife has a heart condition, what the hell are you doing here?"

Andy's face dropped, he felt a cold chill running down his nerves. This wasn't the response he expected. Frank looked angry, was there some unresolved argument between them? Andy couldn't remember anything. No, he must have startled them and Frank was speaking out of excitement. Andy regained his composure.

"I'm sorry Carol, I didn't mean to startle you. I was just happy to see you both," he lifted his basket. "I'm just running a few errands. Picking up some groceries for Edith. Muffins, Mustard, Bread and Pie, oh my." Andy grinned.

At the mention of Edith's name, Carol sank her face into Frank's sleeve and whispered, "Oh Frank." She was sobbing. Frank's expression hardened.

"Edith?" he blurted, "Andy, where's Brian?"

Andy blinked and stepped back, "Brian? My son? Well I expect he's at home with that lovely bride of his getting ready for their first child. She is pregnant, you know." He beamed as a warm sensation rolled up his chest.

Brian had grown to be a fine young man, graduating with an Engineering degree and a good job. He had immediately announced his plans to get his Masters and then sweetened the deal by revealing his plans to marry his lovely girlfriend who was also graduating with a teaching degree. A couple of years later they arrived at the house to announce their news about the baby. Andy was so thrilled he took the whole family out for dinner. That was his proudest moment of all.

"All any parent wants," Andy said to his wife that night, "is to know their children are safe and on the road to fulfillment. Now you can enjoy all those children you wanted so badly." Andy's daydream was shattered with Frank's loud voice.

"For Christ sakes, Andy. What's the matter with you? Why do you keep doing this? Goddammit, where's your son?" Frank's face was blood red as he pulled his sobbing wife behind him in a protective gesture. Confusion started mixing up all the images in Andy's mind. What did Frank mean, keep doing this? A violent shudder rolled up Andy's back, his stomach threatened to erupt as his neck warmed uncomfortably. He looked around at the crowd that was starting to form. He reached for something to hold on to.

"I – I don't understand, Frank. What do you mean? I just came to get some –" Andy tried to back away from the group. He wanted to run, the sickness was taking hold and fear gripped him. His legs were weak and his chest hurt. Frank grabbed his sleeve, cutting off his escape.

"No, Frank. Let me go. I have to -"

"Buy some groceries for Edith. I know, you said that," Frank's voice was like gravel crunching under a tire. "Don't you remember anything, Andy? Do you know what happened to Edith? Do you even know what day it is?"

Carol pulled on her husband's arm, "No, Frank. Don't do that. He's not well."

Andy's head was a carrousel. What happened to Edith? What was wrong? Faces and sounds spun around slipped between the real world and some other one. A dull hum was filling his ears and the sound of Frank's voice echoed in the distance like thunder. Like hammer sounds in a long, deep tunnel. He clung to Frank's hand like a drowning man.

The store manager ran up to the scene with Billy close behind. "What's going on here?"

Frank was trying to pull Andy's hand from his sleeve. "This man is sick. Take him to the office and I'll call his son to get him."

"We should call an ambulance," the Manager suggested.

Frank shook his head, "No, he's done this before. I'll get his son and he'll take care of him."

"But, I don't understand," Andy was pleading, his voice fading. He realized that Billy was guiding him away toward the side of the store where the office was, "I just came to pick up some things. My wife will be -" then the world went white and the roaring in his ears became a calming white noise.

Andy heard Brian's voice through the haze. "Hey Dad, how's it going? I thought I'd stop by," his smiling face floating above, obscured by clouds. As his senses returned, Brian's voice became darker, more agitated. Andy opened his eyes briefly but the bright office lights stung, so he kept them closed. He was lying on a cot of some type. The metal edges pushed into his shoulders painfully but he couldn't move, exhaustion seemed to hold him down like a weight. He tried to understand the voices in the room. Frank was still angry and Brian sounded defensive.

"... went out for a few minutes. He was asleep, I thought he'd be okay."

"You can't let this happen again, Brian," Frank's voice rose in pitch, "He'll hurt himself, or someone else."

"I know, Frank. I'm sorry," Brian sounded tired.

The store manager's voice cut in, "What exactly is wrong with him? I don't understand."

Carol was sobbing, telling Andy she was still there. Brian sighed and a chair squawked as he sat down.

"He was in an accident about a year ago. We were driving home from dinner. We were celebrating my wife's pregnancy, when we were broadsided. I don't know all the details but the police said it was likely the other guy's fault. Anyway, since then my father has lost his short-term memory. He doesn't remember anything after the accident."

A tumult of chaos descended on Andy's mind. A rumbling, screaming riot of noise; confusion, pain and wretchedness. He felt pain returning, threatening to burst his head. "Edith!" He called out so loud the others jumped and Carol cried out. They stared at Andy but he only looked to the ceiling, eyes searching and then closing again.

The store manager spoke, in a whisper, "Is Edith your mother?"

Brian's voice caught as he tried to speak, "Yes, she died in the crash, along with – along with – " Frank put his hand on Brian's shoulder.

"They both lost their wives that night," Frank's voice was calmer, slower, "Andy was in a coma then in some form of semi-consciousness. Brian has had to look after him ever since."

"It was so hard to accept," Carol's voice joined in, still wavering, "They released Andy from hospital but he wasn't himself anymore. We tried to help but he was just too far removed. It was like he was dead, or waiting to die. We didn't think he would make it."

Frank's voice returned with its former growl, "Then about six months ago he shows up at our door with some baking he said Edith had done for us. He had no memory of what happened. Carol just about had a heart attack. She has a bad heart you know. I just couldn't let that happen again."

Andy listened as the story played before him like a radio drama. His chest jerked with sobs as he learned the truth of his life, something his mind had hidden from him in its misguided benevolence. His wife was gone, Brian's marriage and family cut short. He had taken so much from everyone he loved and then hid away in a false, Pollyanna existence. Worse was the fact that Andy realized he had lived through this chain of events before, repeatedly discovering the truth and losing his family over and over and over.

Loss of short-term memory. He mulled the phrase while the voices continued to drone in the distance. Andy knew what that was, he had heard of it happening to others but never fully believing it was real. He understood Frank's anger and Carol's fear and he could hear the frustration in his son's voice. Brian, the promising young mind who had to look after an old fool who'd robbed him of his happiness.

"Alright, Frank. I get it," Brian's voice was raised, "He has to go into a home. I can't live like this anymore either. So don't worry Frank, he won't come knocking on your door anymore."

Chairs moved and Frank spoke quietly, "I'm sorry Brian. I'm worried about Carol, not me. It's upsetting." More movement as Frank and Carol moved toward the door. As they passed, Carol paused and put her hand on Andy's arm. The sensation of touch startled Andy and he looked at her.

"We're so sorry, Andy. We miss her very much." She forced a smile momentarily then walked to the door with Frank trailing behind quickly. A tear rolled out of the corner of Andy's eye.

He wanted to go home, he wanted to grieve his lost wife and make amends to his son. He wanted to live out his life with the full knowledge of what had happened and not have to relive this sick feeling of loss again, but he knew, with the coming of the new day, he would forget it all and relive the horror afresh.

A BLIND BEAR
REBECCA LANFOND

I knock. "Dad!" I shout. I listen closely for any movement from
the other side of the door. There are signs of life: white television
light flickers from the kitchen window, his old truck sits on the
cement pad in front of the house. The bumper is detached and
slants to the left. Rust has corroded parts of the body away. Red
duct tape holds both cab lights together. The small Winnie the
Pooh plush toy hangs down from the rear view mirror just as it
has for twelve years. Junk fills the box: empty coolant jars, and
windshield wiper fluid containers, three spare tires with thick
treads, an old long rusty chain, an air compressor, a dozen
empty pop cans, and a car jack.

I knock harder. Hope helps me believe he did not hear me the
first time.

"Why are you doing this! Come back to the car!" Liam, my
boyfriend, yells from the driveway.

I knock again; my fist striking the door. I stand on the
doorstep and watch the door, unyielding despite my
desperation. I wait, counting all that I have ever known; he will
not answer, but he needs to know I care.

He hasn't answered my calls in the past two weeks. My mind
has made up excuses for him every time he disappears for more
than a few days: did he forget his phone? Is he away from the
truck? Did he get into an accident? Was his body hurled into the
air by a passing car that had failed to slow down? I imagine the
worst as time goes on. I have to know that he is alright in order
to calm my worrisome mind.

Gripping the brown side paneling, I lift myself up onto the
window ledge. I stare into the living room. The light from the
T.V. gives the room a haunting glow. Budweiser bottles and
empty pint glasses litter the coffee table. He sits hunching over
the table; elbows resting on his knees; pinching a cigarette
between his calloused fingers; eyes holding no thoughts – his
mind numb. He lifts the death stick to his mouth and it burns to
life, waking a sleeping dragon. Smoke drifts out of his nostrils,
hovering in the air.

My heart sinks into my soul. A man sits there. A cigarette burns in his hand—always a bad sign. I can't look anymore. I step off the ledge and stand on the doorstep. I do not know this man. I do not want to know him.

As I look at this man sitting alone – imprisoned in a house of memories, trapped with his lonesome thoughts – I am reminded of his recent fiftieth birthday.

We sit on portable lawn chairs in a grassy clearing surrounded by trees. Five chocolate cupcakes sit on a red cooler in front of us while blue butterflies flutter effortlessly about. The leaves have almost finished changing color and the air is a warm wool blanket.

"Happy Birthday, Dad!"

"Thank you, baby. Did you make these cupcakes?" He stuffs a chocolate cupcake into his mouth.

"I sure did. So did Grandma and Grandpa call you today?" I ask and take a sip from my glass bottle of cream soda.

"No, you're the only one I've talked to."

This admittance is a serrated knife in my heart, twisting and tearing it open.

In my earliest memory, I am four years old. I am staring at the ceiling wondering who managed to glue hundreds of popcorn kernels to it. My stomach pinches with hunger. I creep out of my blankets and slide down the chilly aluminum frame of my bunk bed and peek down the hall. Light drifts up from the living room downstairs. Mom and Dad are still up but the taste of Mom's oatmeal cookies gives me the courage to sneak downstairs. I creep down, glued to the wall, walking on my tip toes along the stair ledge, carefully avoiding the creaky parts. I reach the bottom and to my surprise my Mom and Dad are not there. A loud thud arises from the kitchen. I crane my neck around the corner and see Dad's large hands around Mom's slender neck. I think her head might pop off like one of my Barbie dolls. I watch him violently shake her and press her hard against the wall. He is inches away from my mother's beautiful face. "Do you understand me?" He repeats like a broken record. His teeth protrude from his mouth like he is about to consume her. Spit flies from his mouth as his grip tightens. Mom presses the palms of her hands against the wall, trying to push it back; an attempt to get leverage.

He is the monster from my dreams.

Tonight I stand on his doorstep. My blood hardens and I push this man away, I lock him up deep in my heart: a place so far that I will be unable to find him. I push it all away. My hands clench, my knuckles protrude, and my fists vibrate. I want to punch through the door. This door should not exist. I need him to see that I care. I need him to see that I am standing here, waiting. I want to hug this man and tell him I love him, but that cigarette is pinched between his fingers. I know it's best to avoid him in this condition.

I am eight years old and I stand in the middle of the soccer field. Someone kicks the soccer ball from down field and it rolls straight to my feet. A part of me hopes it rolls by but a part of me is ready. Everyone is concentrated on the opposite end of the field, so it is up to me. Somehow the world has brought everything together for this one moment; this is my chance. The ball bounces off my feet. I stand and look at the goal keeper a few yards before me. I freeze in terror.

"Go, baby! You can do it!" My dad screams from the sidelines.

I guide the ball down the field; it's just me and the ball. I swing my leg back, gaining energy for the big finale. My foot makes contact with the ball and it cuts through the air. The goal keeper reaches for the ball but it is no use. I have just scored the winning goal.

Dad blows his air horn and goes wild with excitement on the sidelines, knocking over the lawn chair and annoying everyone in the process – everyone but me. I run into his arms and he lifts me up to the sky. I reach up to touch the sun.

My dad jumps with pride and announces to all that I am his baby.

I've always known he sits in this house by himself, but for years I have not wanted to admit it. If I admit this, I am stuck facing my enemy — guilt. I hold the guilt from the life my parents' once shared; the life that exists within me; the life that flows through my veins. I am those walking memories; the evil ancestors; the unwelcome guests that creep into my mind late at night when it is difficult to fall asleep; those ghosts that reveal themselves when I am most vulnerable. I am those memories that cause this man to sit here utterly alone.

I am five years old. My hair sits on my head like a mushroom cap. I am squishing my toes into the brown shag carpet that smells musty if you press your face into it. My grandparents rush down the stairs holding boxes that my Mom and I packed with my stuffed animals.

"Where's Daddy? Will he be hungry when he gets back?"

Everyone is too busy to hear me.

I walk to the kitchen to make sure the leftover Chinese food is still there for when my Dad returns.

"Don't take this Chinese food, it's Daddy's."

I tell them this as they take the last of the boxes from the front door. I leave my purple candle for him on the T.V. stand. Once it melts there is a tiny angel pendant at the bottom. Dad told me he liked this candle, I figure I will let him have it until I come back from visiting my grandparents.

But I do not return to the house until I am seven years old. He returned to an empty house after a long week of work. All I see is the week old Chinese food and a man with swollen red eyes, sitting alone in an empty house, wondering what went wrong.

He sits here every night. This eats away at me while I sit comfortably in my own home. This reality causes me pain, so I close my eyes. This is all too familiar in ways that until now have been left to my imagination. The reality of this scene startles me as I had hoped deep down that it would not look this pathetic. The familiarity terrifies me.

I step off the doorstep and walk down the sidewalk towards the car. Each step seems to stick to the ground and I have to pry my feet off the cement. My breath flows out of my mouth and up into the night. My body quivers and I swallow, holding the tears in. I clench my fists tighter, digging my nails into my soft, fleshy palms so I may not feel the spiny lump in my throat. My mind races with distant memories that I have been longing to forget.

He stumbles in the backdoor of my grandparents' old farmhouse. My family scatters about like ants hoping the large bully will not torment us today. His work boots stomp into the house and leave a path of dry mud flecks behind him. He staggers in, holding the frame of the doorway, but loses his footing from the kitchen rug. He catches himself on the stove and tries to regain balance with one hand, while a can of Budweiser is glued to the other.

"Where's Gord?" he bellows. His voice is raspy, as if he hadn't slept for days and his smile is anything but welcoming. His blue jean button up shirt is faded from a lifetime of washes and holds fossilized oil stains from his hard lifestyle; constantly replacing parts on his semi; driving hours on end hauling peat moss across Alberta.

"Where's Gord?"

His determination to find Gord frightens everyone in the room so we all remain silent. Earlier that day, Dad had found out Gord, his brother-in-law, had refused to help Grandma and Grandpa during harvest time. My dad has always been intolerant to bullshit. He loves his parents and would do anything for them so he cannot fathom how the rest of his siblings would act otherwise. Since my grandparents, my dad's parents, live in Saskatchewan, he doesn't see them as much as he'd like. If he had the time, he'd help them around the farm as much as he could. When he finds out his family is unwilling to help or blatantly takes advantage of them, it drives him nuts; alcohol and god-knows-what increases these feelings tenfold.

Everyone takes turns looking at each other as if to say "don't say anything — let the moment pass. If we ignore him, he'll go away." Grandpa timidly shuffles into the dining room. Aunty Pam sits at the kitchen table, twiddling her fingers. Aunty Tanya hurries to dish out food for cousin Emmi and shoots me an uneasy smile. I stand next to the kitchen sink waiting to dish up stuffing. I try to look into his eyes but it is no use because I am looking at a stranger. He smells pungent; dirty socks; stale old shoes; harvest time, and a dash of fresh feed. His eyes are foggy, clouded over, so he cannot see what he is doing.

Against all of our best interests, Gord walks into the room, completely unaware of what he is walking into. My Dad is a tall, burly man, very top heavy, so when his fist comes into contact with Gord's face, Gord plunges into the fridge and the mashed potatoes from his plate fly into my face. My father looks down at Gord and spits on him. Grandpa drops his plate and his food paints the dining room floor. Despite his old age he runs into the kitchen and attempts to hold his son back; a natural straight jacket. I stand there watching my Grandpa and my uncles haul this stranger outside onto the porch, his feet scrambling about as he yells profanity. I watch Grandma wince with every slashing word. His mighty roar shakes the kitchen and everyone watches in astonishment, mouths dropping, eyes locked on my father. Food has flown about the room during the ruckus. Gord's mashed potatoes are smeared over the floor along with peas and random magnets from the fridge. Tiny blood droplets stamp the tile. Someone has sat on Grandma's birthday cake in an attempt to avoid the mauling and now it is pancaked over the kitchen table. Grandpa pulls his pants up with his belt buckle.

I stand before the window, completely mesmerized by this creature outside face down on the ground. It takes four grown men to calm him down. The man is so dangerous, so sad. He is a bear that has not realized he is fuzzy and soft. I want to cuddle the bear but he would slash my neck open.

Streams of warmth fall down my face and I realize it is not the mashed potatoes; I am crying. I am mortified. I turn around and everyone in the kitchen is looking at me and then looking at the destruction the bear has left behind. Blood rushes to my cheeks.

"Don't cry, my baby," Grandma says. She gently dabs my tears away with her tea towel.

The drive home from his house tonight is a blur and when we get home I take it off; I take it all off. The water bursts out and shocks me back to life. It engulfs me like a sea of open arms. The water trickles down my body and masks the guilt that leaks from my eyes, washing away all that torments me. The little rivers trail down my arms, down my sides, down my legs, and down into the drain where they disappear. I turn the heat higher and the hot water melts away any leftover feelings; it kills the bacteria that enters the blood stream, weakens the heart, and infects the mind. I cannot hear the outside world and I am safe here. The thick humidity acts as a blanket yet it makes the air heavy which requires me to fight to live; reminding me to breathe; reminding me there's more to life than feeling guilty.

I wake up the next morning and notice a missed call and a new voicemail from my dad. I anxiously punch in the password to check my voicemail and wait eagerly to hear his voice and what he might have to say.

"Hey baby, just giving you a call. It's about seven-forty-five, just heading back into the city now, should be back by eleven. Just wondering if you wanted to go for lunch when I get back. I'll call you a little later. Think about where you want to go in the meantime. Call you in a little bit. Take your time getting up. Dad loves his baby, see ya."

I delete the voicemail and dial his number. The phone rings. I will always call him back. The phone rings again. I will always forgive him. And again – he needs to know I care.

He finally answers. "Hey, baby. I was just about to call you."

I am overcome with an overwhelming sense of relief.

DAMS
NATHAN WADDELL

The best thing about building dams, Billy thought, was that there was always a perfect-sized rock, with just the right shape, to put just where you need it. They didn't fit together as smoothly as Lego, but well enough for his purposes. Just now he needed a rock shaped sort of like Alberta, and soon enough he found one, though it had a little jag on it as if it had a cowlick just like his favorite cartoon robot, Glomulan. Good enough. Billy placed it and watched with satisfaction as his morning labours were completed.

The water built up and then poured over the top with a pleasing shoosh sound. The creek rose perceptibly, though not as high as its spring thaw level. Billy loved how the water flowed over the top layer of rocks, a thin layer of living water that created a thousand tiny waterfalls as it fell into the stillness below. A perfect miniature world. For the rest of the afternoon Billy placed sticks into the pool, so he could throw rocks at them. It was his own version of Battleship, but with less random guessing and more smashing and splashing.

That evening he recounted his adventures to his mom. She remembered what it was like to be a child, so she nodded and clapped and laughed in all the right places. Billy's dad, however, was a much more ossified adult. "You shouldn't leave your dams intact, William. You might divert the stream."

"I'm sure he won't, dear," said Billy's Mom.

"Yeah, Dad, I won't wreck anything." Billy didn't want to lose another of the few activities available to him at their summer cabin in Fort Kurri.

"Because the beavers are always building dams and flooding the stream so the forest rangers have to come and shoot the beavers and blow up the dams."

"They do? That's mean!"

Mom nudged Dad, so he amended himself. "Well, they used to do that in the old days. Now they just, uh, tranquilize the beavers and relocate them to more remote places."

"Like they do with problem bears?"

An Edmonton Anthology

"Exactly. But my point is, be careful you don't fall in the water and get hypothermia."

Billy was pretty sure Dad's point had actually been to stop him from building any more dams, but he knew better than to correct him. "I won't," he promised.

The next day Billy spent time in his tree fort and rode his bicycle. He spent some time looking for beaver dams, but they all must have been blown up since he couldn't find any. After a while he realized he was straying a little too far from home, and the thought of running into a stray bear sent him racing back to the cabin. By the time his tree fort came into view, Billy was being pursued by an entire cadre of bears, chasing him on rocket-powered flying motorbikes. Billy performed a controlled wipeout, sending his bike bouncing against a tree as he rolled and climbed up to his fort in one continuous motion. Once secure in his battlements he aimed his laser cannon at the ursine biker gang and shot them all out of the sky. The cannon was set to "hibernate", of course. Billy was merciful.

He set down his cannon, which had started life as a tree branch he had found and whittled with his dad's hatchet. He looked out the glassless window at Mt. Messier across the lake. Dad said the water from his little creek came from snow melting off of Mt. Messier which in turn filled up Lake Coffey. Dad liked to make up stories but Mom had actually confirmed this fact, which Billy found harder to believe than the story Dad told about carnivorous moose. It just didn't seem like there was enough snow in the whole world to provide water for the creek. He decided to perform an experiment- he would add another layer of rocks to his dam to see how much water would accumulate. Maybe he could break the record set by the spring thaw.

Billy crossed the stepping stones he used as scaffolding. He gathered an armful of likely-looking stones and laid them on top of the dam one by one. It took him almost an hour- the increased pressure of the water kept knocking some of his stones down. Rather than becoming frustrated by this, Billy spent some time holding a stick atop one of the stones to test how much it was pushing. Water, Billy decided, was rude- it didn't just swerve out of the way of obstacles, it tried to shove them out of the way. Billy Scientist eventually made way for Billy Engineer and he finished the project. One of his stepping stones was now submerged so he suffered a wet foot when he recrossed the creek. He decided the foot would become gangrenous if he didn't make it home in under 100 seconds so he took off at full-speed, counting steamboats as he ran. At 103 he staggered in the door, to be greeted by his mom who was reading a National Geographic on the couch.

"What happened to you?" Mom asked. Her son was writhing on the floor.

"Gangrene, Mom. You'll have to amputate."

"Too bad you're not an Amazon tree lizard," she showed him a picture from her magazine. "It says they can regrow their limbs in a couple of months. Well, bring it here and I'll cut it off."

Billy submitted to the surgeon's scalpel. Heroically, he didn't scream. But he did give in to fits of laughter as the surgeon wouldn't stop tickling him.

That night, Billy's mom tucked him in. "Good night, little man. I'm glad your leg grew back already."

"Good night, Mom." Billy shoomped and shwamped until he was good and comfy. "Why doesn't Dad come read me a book anymore for bedtime?"

"Your father is very tired right now, sweetheart. He needs a lot of sleep. But he should be awake in time for breakfast, ok? Get some sleep. Love you." She kissed him on the forehead.

"Love you too."

The next morning, Dad wasn't at the table. Billy felt a little grumpy at this. Mom gave him a bowl of FourGloms, which cheered him right up, especially when the prize landed in his bowl.

"A magnifying glass!" It had a handle shaped like a robot arm with fingers wrapping around the lens. "Just like Glomulan!"

"Now you can be a regular Sherlock Holmes," said Mom.

"Who?"

"Sherlock Holmes! You know, 'Elementary, my dear Watson.' You make an excellent Cumberbatch!'"

Billy screwed up his face at his Mom. "You're weird. I was gonna go look at bugs under logs and stuff."

"Eew! Maybe you're the weird one."

Billy made sure to rinse his bowl out and kiss his mom on the cheek before he ran out to test his new Implement of Unlimited Discovery. Initial experiment subjects were disappointing — diagrams Billy had seen in books had led him to believe the undersides or rocks would be crawling with all sorts of fascinating creatures like millipedes and blind spiders and anonymous little grubs. But all he found was the quickly disappearing end-segment of an earthworm. Disgusted that he couldn't find anything disgusting he pocketed the magnifying glass and headed for his dam.

There was a small boat with a rock or something on it, tapping up against the stones of the dam. Tap tap tap. It was too big to flow over the dam, so it floundered sideways, bouncing and bumping. Billy walked on his stepping stones out to it, kneeled down and scooped it up. Quickly, before he could lose his balance, he hopped back to the bank to study his prize.

The little boat was shaped more like a raft than a canoe- no sides, just a flat surface made of a smooth, fine grained wood. There were two pontoons sticking out for stability, with strange carvings. Even under magnification, Billy couldn't decipher them. But the really interesting thing was the rock lying on top. It laid flat, so it looked just like any old rock, but when Billy picked it up, he saw that it was a geode cut open. Inside were purple crystals, but they had been carved or shaped or maybe just grown somehow into intricate little shapes — a tiny city with walls and towers and little streets, all in purple.

Where did it come from? Billy looked up towards Mt. Messier. Maybe some kid had lost his toy boat? Well, finders keepers. Billy ran back to his tree fort to study the crystalline city more closely. Since he didn't really have access to a mass spectrometer, all he could do was look at it with his magnifying glass. Which was still pretty cool. Eventually, though, he put the geode down and went to ride his bike.

The next day Billy went straight to the dam. There were more little boats floating in the water, gently bumping each other and the edge of the dam. "Sweet!" Billy shouted and he hopped over to retrieve his windfall. Each of the boats were nearly identical to the one from yesterday, but each one carried an unique artifact. One had a tiny scroll, filled with the same sort of indecipherable letters that were carved on the pontoons. Billy could tell it was fancy, but it wasn't nearly as cool as some of the other stuff he found.

One boat had a tiny chest filled with even tinier coins and gems. It was surprisingly heavy. Another had weapons — spears, swords, shields and the like, perfectly sized for his Glomulan action figures. They weren't made of plastic like normal toy accessories. They were sharp. The coolest one of all, however, had a skull on it. It was much smaller than the beaver skull he had found once and that his parents wouldn't let him keep. But it had tusks like a walrus, and four eyeholes.

Billy was ecstatic, but he also wondered where the little boats came from. He no longer thought they belonged to some poor kid. Looking up at Mt. Messier, which today was shrouded in storm clouds, Billy felt a little tinge of trepidation. These little boats shouldn't be here, should they? Briefly he waged an inner argument, but ResponsiBilly lost out (again) to IrresponsiBilly, and he scooped up two of the treasure boats and ran to his tree fort to deposit them, and came back for the other two. By the time he made it back to his fort it had started to rain. HIs mom called him inside.

At supper, Billy's mind was on his secret stash so he didn't pay much attention to his parents. Until his dad said, "William, I know this has been a hard summer for you. I just want to tell you how much I appreciate how patient and understanding you've been with me. I'm sorry I haven't been as attentive to you lately as I'd like."

Though his dad kept talking, Billy was busy trying to figure out how this summer had been hard for him. It was kind of his favorite summer ever. He hadn't even noticed being especially patient and understanding, but he never really noticed half the things he did that got him in trouble so he was just glad that this time he seemed to be in whatever is the opposite of trouble. What IS the opposite of trouble?

"William, are you listening?"

"Yeah, Dad! I'm not in trouble, right?"

"No, William. Billy. Not at all. No. Listen. This operation, it's pretty much just a routine procedure nowadays. They do it all the time, with little, they're almost like little robot arms. Like your Glomuloid toy."

"It's Glomulan, Dad. Robot arms? What are you..? What operation?"

Even though Billy was now fully engaged in the conversation, the barrage of big words that his dad said didn't leave him much wiser. Coronary arteries? Angie O'Plasty? Who's that? And why was she stuffing dad's heart full of kresteralls?

"So… are you gonna die?"

His dad smiled. And sighed. And smiled again. "It's very unlikely, Billy. Not from the angioplasty, at least. I… I'll have to make some changes to my lifestyle, you know, stuff we should all be doing anyway. I have to quit smoking. You've always wanted me to quit smoking. But I have to be honest with you — the blockage is pretty severe. The doctors tell me… they tell me that some people in the same condition I'm in, uh, you know… some people have died."

This was worse than getting in trouble. Way, way worse. Billy wanted to just run away. Go to his room to read comics. Instead he asked to be excused and he went out to his tree fort. The little boats with their sundry cargo were scattered on the floor. Seeing them, Billy realized he didn't really feel like playing with them. And that actually the sight of them just made his tummy feel even more nervous, like maybe how a cat felt when it swallowed a furball that it couldn't cough out.

Billy climbed back down and went around to the front yard to get his red wagon. He gathered all the little boats and put them in his wagon. Looking up at the late summer sky, he figured he still had a bit of twilight left before it got dark. Enough time to do what he wanted. He pulled the wagon to his dam.

There was another boat in the water.

Billy dropped the wagon handle and ran to the water. This boat was different than the others. This one was more truly ship-like, not just a fancy raft with pontoons. Kind of like a miniature canoe, only beefier. With the same letters carved all along its hull. Looking inside, Billy felt a tingle along the back of his neck. There was a little creature inside. Not an action figure. Not a doll. But also, apparently, not alive.

Billy kind of didn't want to look. His heart was beating crazy fast, and his hands were shaking. Finally he told himself to be brave and strong. He looked inside the boat at the body. It was laying peacefully in the little ship, arms crossed, eyes closed. It had blue scaly skin, a slightly turtlish face with spikes around its eyes and mouth. It was dressed in armour and was wearing a tiny golden crown. Next to it was one of those things cartoon emperors always held when they were sitting on their thrones, what was it? A skeptic? Scepter?

"You're a king," Billy whispered.

The boat's progress was impeded by Billy's dam, like the others before it. Billy looked up at Mt. Messier, and down towards Lake Coffey. Whatever land this creature was king of, it wasn't here. Or now, maybe? Billy had no idea. It didn't matter. He knew what he had to do.

He waded into the water. It was cold. Heading for the middle of the stream, he kicked over the Nevada-shaped rock. The Kingboat rode the resulting waterfall easily and floated away downstream. Billy placed the rest of the boats in the water and they followed. He watched them go.

Billy put his foot up on the dam, to the right of the hole he had opened. He pushed with his leg, knocking over a whole big section. The water impatiently roared past him, nearly pushing him in. Angry, he kicked and pushed and swore and yelled until the whole thing was gone, not one rock left where he had placed it.

The best thing about building dams, Billy realized, was knocking them over after they were finished.

HOW TO RUIN A PERFECTLY GOOD FRILLY PINK DRESS

AUSTEN LEE

It begins at the fancy prom dress store, the kind of place that's full of tulle and sequins and you have to take your shoes off at the door. That's it. Go there and find the puffiest, pinkest dress in the room. Try it on. It makes your waist look cinched and the corset pushes your boobs up nicely. Smile, you like it. You're not usually a pink dress kind of girl but you only graduate from high school once, right? It's the beginning of something big — your entire future, the rest of your life. You're going to start out with a bang, and the pink one really does look better than the beige one you tried on before, doesn't it? You're a princess. You're going to shock everyone; they won't see it coming.

It's perfect.

Buy the dress. Pay hundreds of dollars for it and hug your mom because she might be scared and even want to cry, though she hasn't yet. She's holding it in. Hug her anyway, so that she knows you noticed and that you care. You're going to miss her, too.

Next, bring the dress home. Hoard it. Peek at it in your closet and imagine how beautiful and special you're going to look in it and how everyone is going to want to take a picture of you. Go to the bathroom and brush your teeth really hard so they will look perfectly white in all the pictures.

The day will come. Wake up early and curl your hair, stick a thousand pins in it and douse your head in hairspray so that it's so stiff a brick would bounce right off of it, not that anyone is going to throw a brick at your head.

That's just crazy.

Blood. There would definitely be blood. Although a certain amount of bleeding could be anticipated in a situation like that. It would be a brick hitting you, after all. Not like in eighth grade...

You're a woman now!

But don't think about that. Focus on painting your face with sparkly make-up. Be sure to put on just the right amount of eyeliner, ensuring that you look like a princess and not a whore. Blush your cheeks so pink that you look embarrassed. Your face will be red anyway; the blush looks intentional.

Walk into your mother's bedroom. Watch yourself in the mirror as she ties your corset on. Hug her again because she's your mamma and you haven't wanted to call her that since you were five but for some reason you want to so badly right now.

Mamma...

Put on a brave face. Don't cry when your best friend gives her very inspirational and gratifying valedictorian speech, just focus on clutching your hands in your lap hard enough that you can't feel them shaking.

After the ceremony, hug all your classmates, even the ones who you didn't like very much growing up. Let them know that they have shaped you. Feel assured that you aren't going to miss them as badly as you think you will, because soon their names will just remind you of ill-defined parts of faces. These people will eventually become an array of floating eyes and noses in your mind. That is if they had particularly cute and crinkly eyes or particularly crooked and memorable noses.

Your dress is itchy. It's driving you insane but don't take it off. Leave it on all night because your mom paid too much money for it and a lot of people told you that you look lovely and that pink is *so* "your colour." Ignore the fact that you don't really agree. Definitely don't tell them about the beige dress you tried on first. Smile at them instead; your teeth are actually fairly white after all that brushing.

Soon it will be time to go to the dance. Your dad will drive you there. Climb carefully into his truck to be sure not to tear your dress. Inhale the way that the inside of the truck smells: like muddy work boots and diesel fuel and somehow in a way like static electricity. Promise yourself to never forget how much you love that smell. Take a moment to marvel at how it never went away, not even after your dad bought a new truck and didn't get his boots dirty anymore.

Let your eyes fall onto your father's stubbly cheek. Remember how he used to scratch it on your face when you were small, making silly cat noises. It irritated your skin but you still loved it, because it was funny and it made your dad laugh when you laughed.

His stubble never used to be grey.

Go to the hall where the dance is being held. You're exhausted but your hair is still hard and smells like citrus. Buy a drink and drink it fast. Dance with your boyfriend to the crappy music (why is the music at high school dances always crappy?)

Smile at your boyfriend. Do it because he's sweet to you and he wore the pink tie that matches your dress without even saying a word about it. Put your chin on his shoulder and watch your friends on the dance floor. Be looking for that boy who told you he was in love with you that one night when he was drunk, but pretend that you aren't looking for him at all. When he catches you staring, keep your gaze on him for just long enough that he sees your eyes peering into his eyes and then look away. Kiss your boyfriend on the mouth; he tastes like beer. That will remind you — you need another drink.

Go to the bar. The boy will be there. He'll tell you that you look too gorgeous not to dance with him. It's a cheap line, but you'll probably fall for it anyway.

Tell him that there isn't a good song playing, you don't want to dance. Really you'll just feel guilty for staring at him before, and texting him and also sometimes brushing up against him at his locker. But don't say any of that. Just be quiet and let him think about dancing with you.

It will work; he will be thinking about it.

"Too bad about the song," he'll say, and pull you onto the dance floor by the arm. He will spin you so hard that your dress starts to fall down. You'll be dizzy and flying too fast, one wrist in his grip and the other one struggling to hold up the glimmering, beaded corset that is barely clinging to your body. Something bright will strike your eyes; the dress sparkling like a twirling chandelier, and a kaleidoscope of rainbow light beaming at you from the DJ's station.

Tell the boy to stop spinning you.

He will not stop.

Brace yourself, because you're about to whirl around even faster now. You'll spin and spin in circles and even though you'll be laughing in reality you will be scared. Your eyeballs will feel as if they could slip right out of your skull, like two tiny planets shot out of orbit, lost in an abyss of stomping feet and spilled coolers.

"That's enough!" You'll say, still foolishly smiling. Maybe the momentum from spinning is keeping your face stuck that way, because you aren't happy.

The boy will be stepping on bottom of your dress, repeatedly. You'll feel it tearing; the pieces of fabric at the bottom fraying like strings of broken hair. People will be staring.

Then suddenly you won't be moving anymore. You'll be very still. The boy will pull you in close to his face. In that moment you'll be holding onto him, the room bending and contorting around you. Your fingers will dig into his shoulders, gripping the fabric of his suit jacket. You'll notice that he's sweating.

Don't kiss him. Whatever you do, don't kiss him because it hurt the way he was spinning you, tearing your arm out of the socket. It hurt you and he knew it and still he didn't stop. Let your arms fall to your sides. Find your feet underneath you.

Run away. Take off your shoes and run. Pull your dress up. Now the bottom is soaked with spilled beer and vodka.

Go outside. Seek out your friends who always seem to be out there smoking cigarettes. Dry up the alcohol that has stained your now tattered pink frills with the dust from the parking lot. It will look like your body is covered in dirty bubble gum, like someone spit you out of their mouth after you didn't taste good anymore.

Now you can start crying, streak sparkly make-up all over your face. Look like a mess. Feel like a mess. Wait for your boyfriend to find you and then get tears of mascara on his tie. The tie is silk, the stain probably won't come out.

Tell him what happened with the boy. He will be so mad. Hide in the bathroom while he looks around the dance floor to kick the other guy's ass for hurting you.

Stare into the bathroom mirror. See yourself looking like you used to when you were a little girl and you played with your mother's make-up. Florescent lights will illuminate you completely for the first time in hours. *God*, you'll think, it's too damn bright!

Look at your dress. The bottom is destroyed, a tattered curtain.

Call your dad. He'll be there in five minutes; that's what he always says when you call him for help. Believe him, even though you know he will take fifteen. Imagine him flying down the highway in his truck, diesel engine roaring. When he gets there, let him hug you and ask what's the matter. Laugh when he makes a silly joke to make you feel better. It's the only way that he knows how, without getting mad at other people.

This is important: when you get home, be sure to take the pins out of your hair. They'll stab your head in your sleep if you don't. Next put on your pajamas. They're soft and decorated with a pattern: cowgirls riding horses. Let that remind you of your mother. Know that she is already asleep in the other room because it's the middle of the night. She may have heard you come in, and probably you woke her up when you called the house to beg your dad to save you. Anyway, don't check on her. She needs to rest; this day was hard on her, too.

You'll wonder if you're ready—for anything at all. You'll wonder if your life is going to turn out like your dress, wilting on the floor: a popped bubble. Wonder for a moment about whose fingers are responsible for breaking its soft, once inflated flesh. It's okay if you're not ready to admit that your own hand played a part.

The word "spiral" will come into your head, and then, "corkscrew." Take notice, but don't think about spirals or spinning or even screwing for too long afterward. Just don't because you're drunk and it feels bad to think about anything, never mind that.

Close your eyes and press your hands against the wall behind you. Steady yourself. Inhale the smell of your house, even though you don't really know what it smells like yet. One day you will, when you haven't been home for a while. You'll know it then, and it will smell good. For now, just wait. Breathe through your nose.

Ignore that your head is sore and uncomfortably stiff. There will be time tomorrow to wash the hairspray out of your hair, to get in the shower and feel the water running down your neck and shoulders. Soon enough, you'll feel like a waterfall.

When it comes, don't forget that feeling: being naked while the day before is washed away down your back. Focus on it carefully, first with your eyes open, and then with your eyes closed. It is a good sensation, one that you are going to need again.

THE EPICENE'S SMÖRGÅSBORD

BRUCE CINNAMON

It's warmed up this past month. No more vicious wind which licks like whips at exposed skin. No more dawns at 10:00 and dusks at 4:00 and empty eternities of soul-eroding night. Instead we have sunlight that beats down on the city, turning ice-clogged roads into rivers of meltwater. Instead we have air that doesn't flay your nostrils for daring to inhale, but carries a rich bouquet of warm, loamy odours. Especially here.

I'm crouched inside a dumpster behind a Greek restaurant with an elderly Chinese-Canadian woman in downtown Edmonton.

I pick up a granola bar wrapper covered with almond butter and give it to my friend, whose mouldering business cards identify her as Professor Tammy Chang, Department of English.

"To eat is a necessity," she says, licking the wrapper clean, "but to eat intelligently is an art."

She passes me a half-chewed pear, which still tastes sweet and firm. I rustle around and find a piece of baklava stuck to a paper napkin.

Our midday meal has become a ritual of exchanges. At first, when I started wandering the streets aimlessly and came upon this stooped old lady, we were both very cautious. But over the past month we've grown used to each other, sharing this new home.

It's very different than any of the homes I've had before. Gritty. Exposed brick. Open-concept. Subway bread smell drifts up the alley from the fast-food outlet at its mouth. Frank Sinatra croons "My Way" from the speakers of a nearby café. Graffiti adorns the rough walls, declaring such things as "Flames Suck" and "Down with Baby Trudeau," alongside a weatherworn "Eaton's Groceteria" advertisement.

I'm about to resume the Rites of Lunch when a fat white girl in a bright pink winter coat charges into our alley, pursued by a pack of boys. She's about twelve years old, has a maroon backpack bouncing below her cascading ginger hair, and she's wearing clunky rubber boots which are much too big for her.

I register the panic in her eyes as they lock onto mine and then boom she's down, tripping belly-first into a slush-filled pothole. The boys cackle and race towards her.

Without thinking I leap out of the dumpster. I draw myself up to my maximum height—which is not a considerable altitude—hook my fingers through my belt loops, and suddenly I'm an Old West sheriff, ready to lay down the law. I stride past the girl, and I can practically hear the spurs on my cowboy boots jangling. I plant myself in front of her, legs spread, wide-brimmed hat shielding my eyes from the desert sun. The boys scramble to a halt, unsure of this development.

The leader of the pack lets his eyes rove over my body, peeling away the layers of my newly constructed self-image. I snap it back in place and drawl out at them:

"Y'all better clear out now, ya hear? Don't wanna be gettin' yourselves into no trouble."

The boys all look to their leader, waiting to follow his cue. I take a step forward, shifting my hand to my hip, fingers hovering over my holster.

"What part of 'git' don't you boys understand? This here's MY TOWN, and we don't stand for no hoodlums!"

I advance on them, and the boys are spooked. They start inching away, not wanting to wimp out but not willing to get their soft little asses kicked in. The leader notices this and tries to regain control of the scene. He forces a laugh.

"C'mon guys, we've got better things to do than talk to street bums." He looks past me at the girl, who's dripping with muck and glaring at him. "Have fun with your new friend, fat ass!"

The boys strut off down the alley, playing it cool. They glance back as they turn the corner onto the street. The leader gives us the middle finger and his cronies gasp and laugh.

I turn to the girl. She looks at me warily.

"Y'alright?"

I hear the sheriff lingering in my voice and cough it out.

"Sorry. Are you okay?"

She looks me up and down and frowns. I know she's asking herself the same question that everyone asks these days. The question that I fought for so long to keep out of people's minds, until I realized that I enjoyed having it there. That it made me powerful. That it allowed me to experience things most people don't allow themselves to experience.

"Are you a man or a woman?"

I hold her gaze for a moment, then slowly shake my head. "No."

Over the past month I've revolted against my anxieties and embraced the ambiguity of my body. I let my hair go wild and it grew with impossible speed. Now it hangs around my shoulders. I've taken to wearing black, form-fitting clothing that emphasizes certain curves and invents others. When people look at me they frown, and ask themselves the question that I now encourage. Especially white people, who often have difficulty gendering people of colour. And I am brown as the mouths of rivers.

I've found this absence-of-gender to be very useful; I can overlay anything I want onto it, for any context. I imagine myself into a character, and act with the full force and confidence of that new personality. For example, a badass sheriff chasing off some bandits.

I ruffle my feathers and become a fairy godmother, to comfort and delight. The girl's eyes widen at my transformation.

"I used to be a man," I say, leaning back against the dumpster. "Not much of a man, I grant you. I was always too short, too skinny. I couldn't grow a beard. I kept my hair cropped close to my skull so nobody would accidentally 'ma'am' me from behind."

I run my fingers through my bedraggled mane and sigh.

"But I got tired of it. Being a man is so much work. You have to shut down whole parts of yourself, monitor what you're doing just in case it's not a manly thing to do. Don't admit to knowing anything about cosmetics or fashion. Be disgusted by the details of female bodies, even as you crave ownership over them. Don't cry, don't show emotions, don't even admit to having them."

Rush hour traffic grumbles past the alley's mouth. Brisk businesspeople march past, never casting a sideways glance at us. The panting, slush-drenched girl has eyes only for me.

"It was like I lived in a grand palace, but I only ever let myself go into three or four rooms. And I want to visit all the rooms. The study and the nursery, the garage and the kitchen and the library. And to do that, I had to stop thinking about walls entirely."

"All boundaries are conventions, waiting to be transcended," says Professor Tammy, popping her head over the lip of the dumpster.

The girl jumps in surprise.

"Oh yes, this is my best friend Professor Tammy Chang. This is…"

"Diana," says the girl hesitantly. She brushes slush off her coat. It's dirty, but drying fast in the sun. Her face is flushed and sweaty.

Professor Tammy grins at her, and I take her mittened hand in mine.

"I'm very pleased to meet you, Diana. I don't have a name right now, or else I'd introduce myself."

Diana's eyes narrow.

"What do you mean you don't have a name? Of course you do."

"Sometimes it's bad to have a name. Sometimes a name is just a beam from which to hang a noose."

Diana stares into my eyes in an unsettling way. There's something about her intense gaze that boils off all my illusions. I can feel the fairy godmother evaporating from my skin.

I flit away from the dumpster and pirouette around Diana, escaping her gaze and smiling to myself at the feeling of this new mystique.

"No single name could ever capture my infinite variety."

"Other women cloy the appetites they feed, but she makes hungry where most she satisfies," murmurs Professor Tammy, sinking back into the dumpster.

"So… you want to be a woman now?" asks Diana. "Is that what all this has been about?"

"I could be a woman or a man, or something in between, or something totally different."

"Thesis, antithesis, synthesis," Professor Tammy intones, her voice resonating out from the dumpster.

"I move through space and time, and I change forms. I can't think of myself as just 'a man' anymore. That's a lie."

"Unity. Plurality. Totality." Professor Tammy chants.

"It's like when you see a two-dimensional representation of a cube, and you don't know which way the cube really sits, and your mind flips back and forth between multiple interpretations."

"A Necker Cube," says Diana.

"What's that?"

"That's exactly what you're describing. It's an optical illusion that Louis Albert Necker invented in 1832. I read about it on Wikipedia…"

"Yes that's it exactly. I'm like a Necker cube — a three-dimensional object in a two-dimensional context."

I smile at her, impressed. "You're really smart."

She shrugs. "I read a lot. I have a lot of time because I have no friends."

She glances back towards the alley's mouth.

"Why were they chasing you?"

She gives me a sour scowl.

"Are you stupid? Look at me."

Her voice is hard. She's had enough of people pitying her, pretending that they're too righteous to have noticed her body is different, is less than ideal.

"Well they won't be coming back around here any time soon," I say.

"Oh yes they will," she says. "They're like hyenas —"

"They scare easily but they'll be back, and in greater numbers," says Professor Tammy, clambering out of the dumpster.

"Exactly," says Diana.

"Well we better make ourselves scarce then," I say. I go over to our pile of ratty blankets beside the dumpster, grab the big rectangular bag into which I've stuffed my new life, and drag it out into the centre of the alleyway. I lift the top flap and grin up at Diana.

"It's good to have props and costumes before you go out and face the world," I say. "Then people will take your self-image more seriously. They can always see it when you act it, but a little help never hurts."

"The apparel oft proclaims the man," says Professor Tammy, selecting a clip-on bowtie from my tickle trunk. "Naked people have little or no influence on society."

She shuffles over to her favourite piece of cardboard.

Diana looks apprehensively at the nest of blankets, the magazine cut-outs stuck to the walls around Professor Tammy's den, the mouldy pile of books next to her bed.

"So you really are street bums…"

Professor Tammy scoffs, and leans back against her oil drums luxuriously. "I choose to live my life on my own terms, and in surroundings with which I can identify. That is the privilege of wealth." She adjusts the tattered old Oilers jersey she's wearing with dignity.

"Come on Diana," I entice. "Take a mask. Come on an adventure with us."

Diana hesitates, then leans over and starts rooting around for a costume.

"This bag really smells," she says.

"Yeah, it used to hold a bunch of sweaty stuff… never mind. Take anything you want."

She selects an enormous pair of sunglasses. I take out a tiara and a sparkling wand.

"Now," I say, "if I could grant you one wish, what would it be?"

"I don't know," says Diana.

"Of course you do. Just tell me."

I swish and flick my wand back and forth, waiting patiently. Diana watches me for several moments, weighing whether or not if she'll indulge me. She crosses her arms.

"Not that it matters, but if I could really have any wish, I would wish to get out of here. Not just this alley I mean, but get out of Edmonton."

"And where would you go?"

"Phoenix," she says immediately.

"Why Phoenix?"

She shakes her head.

"Nevermind. No reason. Forget I mentioned it."

Suddenly she seems agitated. She takes off the sunglasses and sets them back in the bag.

"I should probably get going," she says.

"We should all get going," I say. "We should fly to Phoenix, and quickly."

Diana rolls her eyes.

"Look, thank you for helping me get away from Brendan and them. But I really need to go. Not to Phoenix, just home."

"What's so great at home?" I ask.

"Don't tell me not to fly," says Professor Tammy, "I simply got to."

"Professor Tammy is right," I say. "If ever you're unhappy with things, one of the best solutions is to seek green pastures elsewhere. You can become a new person in a new context."

Diana looks around at the melting alleyway, then shakes her head.

"We can't go to Phoenix," she says. "We don't have passports or any money."

"Well fine, but least come with us on a little adventure and we'll see where we end up"

Diana scrutinizes me with that laser-sharp intensity, then finally nods.

"Fine," she says. "I've nothing better to do."

"The world is not yet exhausted," says Professor Tammy, sweeping her arms around us. "Let me see something tomorrow which I never saw before."

When on an urban odyssey, meanders are not only enjoyable, but necessary. As the sun fades out and the streets clear of commuters, we tramp around downtown. We soak our feet at the base of the Citadel's indoor waterfall, and warm our hands at the bonfire in front of city hall. We walk past the mangled silver ruins of the art gallery, which was dynamited by art terrorists a year ago and still hasn't been fully cleaned up. We wander past the Harbin Gate, beg some fortune cookies off a tough old restauranteur, and we all swap fortunes when we find we like each other's more than our own.

"We could go by Katz Place," says Diana.

"I try to avoid the arena," I say. "I don't like that neighbourhood."

She casts a sideways glance at me. "Don't you like seeing all the holograms replaying last night's game on the plaza? I know it's kind of cheesy, but they're fun to watch and walk through."

"Let's just go down Jasper Ave," I say.

As we walk down Edmonton's main street, we draw stares from the pedestrians around us. I feel the curious glances as people see my form flickering back and forth between two interpretations. A car races by, trying to pass another along the curb, and we dance back from the tsunami of slush its tires throw up onto the sidewalk.

Next to me, Diana pushes her sunglasses up her nose and lifts her head up higher. I see her subtly turning her head, noticing all the people who are watching us.

"For a while," I tell her, "I was a reverse-pickpocket on the LRT. I spent all day slipping fifties into people's pockets. That was near the beginning of my adventures."

"How did you get the money?" she asks.

"It was leftover from a long-ago life I gave up so I could enjoy adventures like this. No more money, but now I have an abundance of time."

"*That* is the privilege of *wealth*," says Professor Tammy.

We pass a Second Cup, and a bunch of teenagers in the window stare out at us. A bus drives by, and several people do double takes at us we disrupt their lazy gazing out at the familiar street. We are bright sparks in a grey landscape.

"What life are *you* trying to leave behind?" I ask Diana, eager to change the subject.

She sighs and the rock-star aura imbued by her sunglasses fades a little.

"Every day after school I go to Arby's and have a Beef 'n Cheddar sandwich and read Wikipedia articles until my mom has gone home from work and gone out again. Then I get an Orange Julius and take the bus home and watch the game, or play Xbox. That's my life."

"But not today."

"Today Brendan and his friends saw me in the food court."

We turn off Jasper Avenue, start walking south to the bridge.

"They don't like me because I'm smart and not pretty. Isn't that dumb? If I were pretty, they would be intimidated by how smart I am and want to impress me. But they see my fat, and they shift inside from being impressed to being annoyed. 'Oh,' they think, 'who does this fatty think she is? Why should I listen to her? What does she know about anything? She can't even control herself enough to not stuff her fat face!'"

Diana's face has gone red, and her voice catches.

"Well fuck 'em," I say. "I'm impressed. Not many people would be brave enough to come on an adventure like this. Most people are too prejudiced."

We walk out to the middle of the bridge, where wind carried along by the river howls at us. Chunks of ice float downstream. The setting sun brushes long streaks of orange-gold pigment across their white canvasses. Soon the night chill will descend on Edmonton, and freeze it all over again.

"Maybe they're right though," says Diana as we lean against the rail and look out. "Maybe I am annoying. I do think I'm smarter than them, and I don't try to hide it. I know I'm fat and ugly, and I won't delude myself into thinking I'm not."

She sighs and looks down at the river far below.

"Maybe I do belong here."

She turns her blistering gaze on me, vaporizing the fairy godmother with a single arched eyebrow.

"Maybe when we pretend about ourselves, when we imagine fantastic things, we're just avoiding the truth of our situations. And the truth is that this is an ugly city, full of worn-down, faded-out people."

I open up my bag, take out a chunky gold ring I acquired recently.

"Or maybe it's full of diamonds in the rough," I say. "Of geodes waiting to be split open, unaware of the thousand glittering surfaces inside of themselves." I take off one of her Team Canada mittens and slide the ring onto her finger. I can feel the heat radiating from her stout little body.

Just then some lights pop on down in the river valley. We all turn to look instinctively.

"Of course," says Diana. Her arm lances out at the glowing building on the riverbank. "That's it! There. That's my revised wish."

The Rossdale Tea Experience opened its doors only a few months ago, and has since endured a constant stream of cries to shut it down. An eccentric billionaire named Eugene Fulgens purchased the old Epcor Power Plant from the City of

Edmonton, offering them a price they couldn't refuse. To the
frustration of his apparent heirs and to city planners eager to
tear the building down, Eugene Fulgens bequeathed his entire
fortune to a foundation which set up the Rossdale Tea
Experience as his grandiose mausoleum.

Strung with strands of fairy lights and a million Christmas
tree ornaments across the ceiling, the tea gardens are bathed in a
warm, nostalgic glow. The lights snake out of the building's
windows, tangling across its roof and dripping down its sides,
twisting up the abandoned smokestacks which knife the night
sky. Depending on your point of view, the result is either a
magical, whimsical bright-spot in an otherwise drab landscape,
or a gaudy, light-polluting eyesore.

We arrive at the glowing building's entrance to find a black-
vested host with a woolly white moustache standing at a lectern.

"Good evening ma'am—er, excuse me, sir, er," the host
stumbles through titles, then grits his teeth and stops
awkwardly. "Do you have a reservation?"

"No," I say, "but we'd like to go in."

He casts an appraising eye over us and arches an eyebrow.
"We have a dress code."

"Ah!" I pat my bag. "That won't be a problem. Just a
minute."

I toss down my bag and we dig through it again. I select a
green vest with pearl buttons, perfect for emulating an English
Earl. Professor Tammy shimmies into a tweed jacket which
complements her bow-tie perfectly, and Diana takes off her
mittens and bulky pink coat and slips on some white opera
gloves.

"We'll go through now, my good man," I pat the host on the
shoulder as we go past. "Keep my bag will you? There's a good
chap." He nods deferentially. We walk inside, and Diana gasps.

When the power plant was decommissioned they demolished
everything inside of the building, leaving only the outside shell
standing. This demolition included all the plant's floors, all the
way down to the third sub-basement, which means that the giant
room which now functions as the Rossdale Tea Experience
extends some fifty metres below street level, down into the
riverbank. Upon entering this massive space, one can't help but
feel awed.

We make our way down a red-carpeted spiral staircase to the tea gardens. At the bottom there is a sign: "Please remove your shoes and enjoy the grass between your toes." The room's floor is freshly turfed every week, and green grass covers it entirely. We slip off our shoes. The grass is magnificent after the long winter. Our feet were starved for its touch.

"Shall we take a table?" I ask. "It looks like we have our pick of the lot."

The Tea Experience was the toast of the town, or at least a popular eccentricity, when it opened. Now they're struggling to fill tables. Several scathing reviews by prominent food critics halted the flow of customers. The critics' main concern was with the absurdity of serving high tea as a 24-hour buffet—making one of the most decadent and posh meals feel like a continental breakfast at some cheap motel. But most controversial is the tea feast's centrepiece.

In the middle of the giant room, surrounded by white wooden chairs and garden-party tables set with flickering candles, the body of Eugene Fulgens lies in a crystal case. The buffet is spread around him—stacks of cakes and scones, bowls of clotted cream and honey, endless samovars of tea.

"I think we're the only people here," says Diana as she cranes her neck to look around the room. "Yep, I think it's just us—oh wow...."

I follow her gaze and notice the far wall. "Whoah."

The destruction of all the floors didn't prove a problem for the interior designers charged with creating the Rossdale Tea Experience to Eugene Fulgens' specifications. They just built the spiral staircase down from the entrance to the ground floor. But when the city safety inspectors examined the superstructure, they discovered that the building's gutting had significantly weakened the support for the riverside wall. Their objections were silenced with envelopes of cash, and the fancy tea gardens opened on schedule.

We walk up to the riverside wall. It has an enormous vertical crack down its centre, with tons of tiny cracks branching out from it. As per the wishes of Eugene Fulgens, there are thousands of pieces of paper stuck to this wall—prayers to the river, to maintain the integrity of this vast room and to bestow us with its blessing. This dubious engineering strategy seems fun, so we take some of the paper and pens from a nearby table, and contribute our own prayers to the wall.

Turning our backs on the wall proves surprisingly difficult, so we back away slowly before we continue to explore the room. We wend our way through the tables, confirming that we're the Tea Experience's only customers tonight. In the far corner, we discover another surprise: "Please Do Not Play On The Turbine Wreckage," says a sign in front of some red velvet ropes, behind which a twisted pile of metal has been shoved into the corner. A giant gilded clockwork music-box sits beside the wreckage. I go over and wind it up, and a familiar waltz starts tinkling out into the room.

"Well," I say, "Shall we get some tea?"

"I'm starving," says Diana, then blushes. "I mean yeah, I could eat."

We return to Eugene Fulgens and load up. We make several trips back and forth to a nearby table before we settle in to our tea feast. I'm about to take my first sip when I have a better idea: "A toast!" I raise my glass. "To Diana, new friend and adventuremate. I think I speak for Professor Tammy and myself when I say that this has been the best day ever."

"SWITCH PLACES!" shouts Professor Tammy, and Diana and I both jump. "Huh huh huh," she laughs huskily at us, and adds more almond milk to her tea.

I take a sip of my Earl Grey. I scarf down some baked goods and smile up at Diana. She hasn't touched her food.

"What's wrong?" I say through a mouthful of raspberry pie.

"It's just, I've been waiting for the right moment… but I guess now is as good as ever."

Diana pulls her maroon backpack out from under the table and sets it on the grass. She unzips it and takes out a thick navy blue binder with a familiar crest on the front, a teardrop of oil. She flips through pages and pages of laminated hockey cards, showing a panorama of all different sorts of men—some famous, most forgotten.

"My dad and I used to have season tickets. We wanted to collect all the players, every single one since the team was founded back in 1971. It was our special historical project."

She flips to the back and slips a card out of its plastic sheaf. It's signed.

"This is you, isn't it?"

A little man grins up at me, posed with his stick out in front of him.

"No. Not anymore."

I run a grubby finger over the card's glossy surface, smudging the little man's face.

"No. It never was."

I try to hand the card back to her but she won't take it. I put it in my pocket.

"I knew it was you since I first saw you. I pretended I didn't because you were pretending too. And I really liked you. You were our favourite. We liked you best because you proved everyone wrong. You weren't big or strong. You weren't what a hockey player is supposed to look like. But you were smart and quick, and held your own."

Diana stares at me unflinchingly. I sigh.

"It's true that I used to be part of a theatrical troupe called The Edmonton Oilers. Every night we'd put on performances — always the same show, but with some room for improvisation like any spectacle. We were well-received both locally and internationally. I remember putting on my costume and getting into character with my cast-mates before every show, waiting in the wings as the theatre darkened and the audience roared in anticipation, then rushing out onto the stage to begin the first act."

I smile wearily at my two friends.

"It was fun, for a while. But I had to get out of there. "

Diana stares at me unsympathetically. Accusatively.

"So you just left. Just like that."

"I had to."

"Why?"

"It was costing me too much to stay. I was destroying myself. Lopping off bits of myself. I needed something new."

"*I've* lived a life that's full," says Professor Tammy. "I've travelled each and every highway."

"But when you've committed to something, you need to stay with it," says Diana, her face reddening, her voice quaking. "You can't just run off. You can't just *disappear*. That's selfish. That's cruel to the people you're leaving behind. You're just discarding them from your life like they're garbage!"

She takes a long quivering breath. I can hear her heart pounding. I suddenly understand.

"He died, didn't he? Your dad"

Diana looks down at her binder, talks into it.

"No. He moved. A month ago."

"Oh. Phoenix."

Diana blushes to the roots of her ginger hair.

"He left. Just left. Just went."

She grabs her tea and shakily adds a spoonful of sugar to it. Her cup rattles in its saucer. I can still feel the sharp edges of the hockey card on my fingertips.

"So you knew who I was all along?"

She nods.

"You stayed with me today because you wanted to see what I would do?"

She nods again.

"Are you going to tell anyone?"

She stares into her tea for what feels like an hour, and eventually looks up at me. Her eyes are deep and sad. She shakes her head.

"Thank you."

She shakes her head again.

"I just don't understand," she says. She rubs her eyes with the heels of her hands, and looks up at the Christmas-light-strung ceiling. "If someone like you can be so unhappy that you have to run away, what hope is there for the rest of us?"

"I don't know," I say.

We feast on in silence, but I've lost my appetite. After a while, I turn to Diana.

"The only thing I know is that today was a great day, and if I hadn't left my old life I wouldn't have been able to do any of it. You have to realize you're starving before you can be bold enough to taste all the flavours of life. If you want to go to Phoenix, go to Phoenix. Sounds like the perfect place to start a new life."

I see a flicker of hope in Diana's eyes for just a moment.

"I can't," she says.

"Maybe not yet. But soon you must. Don't starve yourself, Diana."

Professor Tammy nods, speaks through a mouthful of cake:

"Life itself is the proper binge."

Untitled
HAYDEN WEIR

A single match

It may burn if only for a second
But in that second something amazing happens

From nothing
appears a flame

A light emerges from where darkness
Only moments before
   Stood
Gracing the universe with untold
Energy
Power
Heat

     Life

For a flame is a live entity
Burning and consuming that which
   Sustains it

Rather like the inside of my mind

A conflagration
Brimming with untold danger
Twitching with animalistic desires
   Destructive
     Untameable

But unlike my mind
A flame can go
   Out
This match

Singular in its existence
Carries with it a
Story

Of
  Memory
Of
  History
Of
  Existence

And when that story has been told
Of
  Endings

      Peace

This combination of wood and sulfur has
Its own mind
Its own soul
That is given oxygen to feed its lungs
Just once before it is killed
By starvation

And it is in this moment that I realise
That I envy that which I hold

Its life is short
Beautiful

And when it has finished burning bright
It's meaning to the world gone
I can crush the life out of it
With no sense of guilt

My mind gives me no
Happy endings
No release from guilt

I receive no peace

I wish I were a match
To feel no pain
To feel no anger
To feel nothing
To only exist

And when my purpose is complete
To be destroyed
Lain to rest
With no regrets

URSUS ARCTOS HORRIBILIS OR BRUCE: A HUNTER'S TALE

TIMOTHY D. FOWLER

The fire is perfect now. The wood I chopped last night into pieces the size of celery sticks burn quickly to perfect cooking coals. I smile to myself while threading last year's moose sausage on a six-foot poplar stick with a prong at the end. This stick, cut with the folding buck knife my grandfather gave me when I was six, used for just this purpose. Sitting here on a chunk of spruce log, I recall the day between Christmas and New Years when the whole family ground, seasoned, mixed and stuffed hog casings in my garage, pinching and twisting them into the moose links now on this stick. I remember these moments and string them together like pearls on a necklace. Each experience stands on its own beauty but strung together — it's stunning. When I stop for lunch, this is the kind of stuff I think about. You could say I am threading a necklace of hunting experiences. The trouble with hunting by yourself is that you are the only one experiencing the necklace being threaded, and no one believes you when you tell them about the pearls. I hunt often on my own. I wonder…Will they believe me? Will YOU believe me?

My sausages are browning up nicely, sizzling, and nearly done.

This is a complicated story…the story of Bruce and me. How we met and made a life together. Why I moved to the country. It's the story of uproar with the press and neighbours. And why I still drive a Ford one-ton pick-up. Not everyone approves of our relationship.

I hunt. A lot. It's tough to find a hunting partner that can keep up with my calendar, selection of tags, multiple seasons and variable tactics—often I hunt alone. There are times I prefer the solitude. First of all, I prefer quiet; second, I eat what I want, when I want; and third, I go where and when I please. All of the choices are up to me. No need to reach consensus on anything. The singular downside is not having anyone to share stories with as the fire burns down to coals long after the sun sets. I guess too, you could add not having anyone to bail you out if you find yourself in some peck of trouble.

Three years ago, just after I bought my new truck, I was up north hunting the second elk season in the balsam forest without much luck. I punch a deer tag the first afternoon and hang the carcass in the shade next to my canvas tent a good ten feet from the ground. The next morning starts with scraping frost off my quad before heading into the woods for a patchwork of walking and sitting. I sit looking over a previously productive cutline and experience what people often describe as *something watching them.* I feel this now. I use my binocular diligently but find nothing. No one is watching me as far as I can see. I sit another half hour or so, breaking down every angle of view for each of 360 degrees. Twice. Nothing. No beady eyes, no hot smelly breath, no mumbling hunters in orange, no cats or wolves. Nothing. I get up and walk a mile or so, find an acceptable vantage point and sit again. There are elk tracks like a path in the brown grass across a schoolyard and elk droppings scattered everywhere like spilled jelly beans.

I hear a clear crack within seconds of sitting. And feel the eyes again. The hair on my neck is twitching and rising. I look and search the surrounding circle, slowly and completely. Again, nothing. I move, find a broad tree stump and sit, looking carefully into the spaces in the dense trees. The feeling of being watched intensifies. Someone, some *thing* is watching me, closer now. Maybe I should work a little harder at getting a hunting partner that can keep my schedule. I hoist my pack, hooking the belt around my middle, and check my rifle. Loaded. Good. Off I go, compass set for the quad. Once at the quad, I reset for the tent and lunch.

A cheery fire is a confidence builder, especially on a dreary day or one where you aren't too sure of yourself. But today the sky is cobalt clear, the wind crisp and easy, and the sun sparkling bright. I build a fire big enough to bolster my confidence and pull up a folding chair with a cup of coffee and contemplate my morning. What was that? Am I imagining things? It would be good to talk to a hunting partner just now. I know they would say, *Don't worry about it. It happens all the time even to me. You'll be fine. It will pass.*

But it doesn't pass. It gets worse. I set my second cup of coffee down empty as the fire eases to coals and step in the tent to retrieve a couple of sausages, returning to the fire to roast them. A twig cracks, and I hear a part moan part growl, then snuffling. It's from the other side of the tent.

I call out. "Hey there!"

More snuffling and moaning. I grab the rifle, prop my sausages against the stone fire circle and stalk around the tent, slowly, thumb on the rifle safety, raising the barrel.

"Hello!"

I round the first corner of the tent. Nothing. Around the next corner, still nothing. Now on the back side of the tent facing the bush looking and listening. A crack and another. Shouldering the rifle, I jump around that last corner to see a ball of fur disappear into the evergreen tangle. My stick of sausages is gone.

See, there was something. Well, at least I am not losing my mind. Or am I?

I find another poplar sapling and cut a replacement stick. Taking my rifle with me, I retrieve another couple of sausages and fixings to redo my lunch. I check the rifle again—still loaded—setting the rifle down within arms reach. My lunch proceeds without incident, as does the rest of the day.

That night, from the comfort of my Coleman camp cot and sleeping bag, I contemplate the day. This is a comfortable resting place, on the precipice of sleep. The cot is a gift from my brother and sometimes hunting partner. I have been comfortably sleeping on this cot for ten years. Ten successful hunting seasons. How many tags have I punched after spending the night on this cot? I tally Mule Deer, White Tail, Moose, Antelope, Black Bear and Elk...I lose count at 47. Thinking about what stole my sausages, I go to sleep.

Snuffling. The first thing I wake to is snuffling. In one fluid motion, I flip my sleeping bag open, grab the rifle and pull back the tent flap. Now the snuffle faces me like it is trying to smell my identification. The sun isn't up but the sky is starting to brighten. I shoulder my rifle, center the scope on the middle and click the safety off. It looks right at me. I imagine it says, "Seriously, you would kill me before breakfast?" We stare at each other, no blinking for three minutes. The milk chocolate fur-ball turns, takes a couple of steps toward where the fire–and my sausages – was yesterday, sits, and makes himself comfortable.

Speaking of breakfast, I could use a little.

"Okay then, I'll make some breakfast for us," I say and take the rifle with me to retrieve bacon, onions, potatoes and eggs. And bread for toast.

Fur-ball sits patiently, watching me place kindling, twigs, split wood and logs to build a fire. He extends his pointy nose and perks his ears when the bacon hits the cast iron, sizzling and smoking, and again when I crack a half dozen eggs in the pan, one at a time with one hand. I cook him four – he seems hungry. I ask him how he slept. I ask where he slept. I ask how long he has been sleeping here. Of course he doesn't answer, at least not exactly. He does watch me carefully. His ears roll and twitch as I talk, big black eyes intent. He seems polite enough and waits for his eggs to cool. He gets the bacon off the plate without tipping it over.

It feels good having company for breakfast. Breakfast pan cleaned, it is time to hunt the morning. I ask him if I will see him later, but he just wanders off. He looks back over his shoulder as he disappears into the bush. I wave.

"See ya' later," not sure if I would.

I return from the day of sitting and walking, and there he is, by the fire pit, on his haunches.

"Howdy! Ready for dinner?"

It seems he is. He watches me do the same fire routine as breakfast. Tonight's cast iron delight is hamburger helper made with venison cut from the carcass hanging behind the tent, coconut milk, fresh green onions, red peppers and mushrooms. I make a double batch. He eats the whole thing, save a plateful for me.

By the time you eat two meals with somebody, you should be on a first name basis.

"Do you wanna be Bruce?" I ask him, looking straight in his eyes. Bruce suits him I think, or at least me.

Bruce and I eat meals together that whole week, just breakfasts and dinners. In spite of no real conversation, I feel there is a comfortable communication between us, and I must say we enjoy each other's company. It is sometimes lonely in the bush, for him too I think. I wasn't looking forward to heading out that final day. The last day of a hunt I normally hunt until noon, make lunch, pack up and head home. This hunt would be the same.

The morning hunt is uneventful. I return to camp to find Bruce in his regular spot, build a small fire and make us some lunch. After a cup of coffee (Bruce doesn't drink coffee) I pack up the tent and the rest of my gear on the small utility trailer. I walk to the creek, retrieve enough water to quench the fire and get back to find Bruce sitting in the box of the 350. Clearly he isn't prepared to say goodbye. Truth is neither am I.

Bruce lies in the back of my truck and sleeps the whole way home. He perks up when I stop to get multiple bags of dog food—hope he likes lamb. We get home. He heads into the backyard, has a powerful sniff of the fenced perimeter, finds a comfortable spot under the cedar and falls asleep in the shade. I find a couple buckets, put food in one and water in the other. I think that I probably need to set up some kind of automatic water and feeder for him. In the late October afternoon he gets up, makes a big stretch and a sort of roar, saunters over to the food and devours the whole thing. I refill and he has another go. Then he finds his previous spot and lies down. We both call it a night.

I am surprised to find Bruce sound asleep at 10 a.m. I poke him with my rake handle, and he doesn't twitch and continues to snore as loud as my first husband. I do a bit of research and find that this time of year animals like Bruce often sleep a lot. He rouses late in the afternoon to consume a huge helping of lamb kibble and takes a big slurping drink. He heads back to the cedar. I notice he is barely visible underneath the cedar, hollowing out a spot to get further into the soil. I can see his middle rise and fall ever so slightly, the snoring stops.

The next day he doesn't rise until dinner time. He quickly eats and returns to bed. The next day I go looking for him at the end of the day, just his nose is sticking out of the hole that swallows him. That is a fine feat of engineering, I think. Three days pass before I see him again.

A week later we have two feet of snow, and there are no tracks in the backyard. I get the rake and a flashlight. I poke a hole into the space where I think he is and shine a flashlight into his face. He is buried deeper now, and his eyes are dreary. He looks up for a brief moment and flops back down closing his eyes.

I don't see him again until spring.

The week after he came out of his den, he ate a truck load of dog food and growled across the fence at the neighbours. I got home from work to find a written complaint in my mailbox, a citation from animal control stapled to the fence and a fine from Conservation taped to my front door. All three told the same story: they didn't approve of Bruce.

The spectacular uproar that followed nearly separated us. It is hard to sort out who was angrier: the hunters who accused me of cheating because I had a super hunter for a partner; the hunter-haters who wanted to stop both of us from hunting; the Conservationists who said Bruce was wild and should be left in the woods; or the neighbours who just didn't or wouldn't understand our relationship.

Bruce and I talked it over that night around the fire in the backyard, after the pretty newscaster left in the black van with her crew, camera and bright lights. She wanted to pet Bruce. Can you believe it? I paid the fine, apologized to the neighbours and we moved to the country. We figured that would suit us both. Now I have a hunting partner that keeps up with my schedule, eats my cooking without complaining and keeps the wolves away.

I am still shaking my head. She wanted to pet him for crying out loud! Everyone knows you don't PET a Grizzly Bear!

But when I tell this story, some folks won't believe it.

RUN IT
AUSTEN LEE

The boy stood in the middle of the street. His bicycle had been discarded somewhere on the sidewalk behind him, beading and dripping water off every dented angle of its composition. They weren't new dents. The bike was old; it used to belong to Tom, before he outgrew it. Isn't it strange how people just stop growing one day?

The boy's eyes were fixed on the pavement in front of him. It shimmered with the downpour of rain, illuminated by the stoplight overhead. Colour spilled onto the concrete, crawling toward him: green, yellow, and red. He was a mirror to each shade. The light was one with his body, shining off the wet surface of his skin.

Red.

The boy did not live near the traffic light. It had been a long bike ride to get to it, the rain sharp on his face, poking him like freezing needlepoints until eventually his skin was numb. Now he was only just beginning to regain sensation. Rain soaked his hair and ran down his forehead, dripping off his nose.

His hands were in his jean pockets. The wet denim was tight on his knuckles and left sore indents on his skin, but the boy did not have the inclination to move them. He simply watched the light bleed onto the pavement, waiting for a car to appear and force him out of his trance.

So far there had been nothing.

And the light was still howling, "Stop!"

It had been that way for too long. The boy wondered if the lamp had stopped working. His eyes flicked up to look directly at it, unmoving and dripping large droplets of water from its rectangular surface. The colour red burned a part of him that was buried somewhere deep inside. He squirmed, but the burn did not go out, nor did the rain lessen it. The boy urged the light to change.

"Turn green," he said, but the lamp did not respond.

"So time's stopped, then?" He went on, "I can do anything I want. I'm the only person left in this whole wide world!"

He was quivering, child-like. When he spoke, laughter was present in his voice. He felt it creeping up into his throat, lodged in his airway like he was choking on a hard candy. It tasted like burnt caramel and broken teeth; he ran his tongue along the inside of his mouth.

He had the world to himself, but the boy still did not move from his place in the center of the street. He would stare down that traffic light for the rest of his life, he thought. Until it gave back what it had stolen from him.

Red.

"I'm not going anywhere!"

The light did not answer. Its reflection on the pavement seemed liquefied, melting into the street.

Then all the boy could think about was ice cream. He imagined a hot fudge sundae, with a cherry and caramel. Sweet caramel, not like the metallic tasting stuff that was currently lining the surface of his throat. Wouldn't he kill for an ice cream sundae right now? Wouldn't he just die for the chance to go for a drive with Tom to Dairy Queen? Tom would get a dip cone. He always did.

There was that urge to laugh again. A sound leapt out of the boy's mouth, but it was not laughter as he had expected but instead a strange wail. He felt his face scrunch up and fire scorch his cheeks. Maybe he was crying. The boy didn't know; his face was wet already from the rain. He didn't press the question too much, chose not to think about it.

"Don't think about it" had recently become his motto.

Yellow.

Why had the light turned yellow? Green came after red. Time must have started to move backwards. Or had his eyes just been closed for a while?

The boy bit his lower lip, a little too hard. He was impatient. His fingers wriggled in his pockets, and he removed one hand from his jeans to wipe his nose. His skin felt the cool relief of fresh air.

"Time does not go backwards," he said.

Though he wished that it did. If there was any moment that the boy would have reversed — stopped in its tracks like a stoplight stops traffic — it would be the event that had occurred in this intersection. When had it been, exactly?

The boy glanced at his watch. It was an expensive one, the kind that showed you the date as well as the time. He'd gotten it for his fourteenth birthday. It was still ticking. The glass wasn't even cracked.

3 months and 9 days ago.

Was that all?

3 months and 9 days ago, the idea had seemed courageous, exciting. They were running late. Where had they been going?

The hospital, the boy thought.

But no, that was where they'd ended up.

3 months and 9 days ago, the boy had sat in the passenger seat of his brother's truck. The radio had been on. He remembered what song had been playing, heard it echo around the empty intersection.

3 months and 9 days ago, the stoplight he stood before now had been red. It had been red as fire truck toys, or birthday cake icing, or a scrape on the knee. It was like the cartoons of The Flash that he used to watch on Saturday mornings: a flying, red blur.

"Just go! Run it!" He'd said, like he was brave.

His brother was older. He was cool, right? He ran it. You bet he ran it. He ran it fast, like in a movie. Oh, it was fast all right. In the blink of an eye they were spinning, like the planet was set on fast-forward. Something had hit them, hard, on the driver's side. Then the boy couldn't breathe. He'd closed his eyes; he was there again.

"Coward," he said to himself now. "Open your eyes."

He did.

Yellow.

Something glittered on the pavement in front of him. Glass. It was the glass from the windshield of his brother's truck. He knew it was. There were just a few shards, what had been left behind when the town crew had cleaned up the street.

The memory of the sound of shattering glass transported him, but not to the moment of impact. It took him somewhere else, to a place that existed beyond the confines of his brother's spinning vehicle.

He was holding a baseball bat. It was heavy and too big for him; his scrawny arms had to fight to keep it upright over his shoulder. Tom was standing in the grass across from him, in front of their childhood home. He was smiling.

"You ready?" Tom shouted.

The boy nodded and got ready to swing, planting his feet on the ground. Then Tom wound up and the baseball came soaring through the air. The boy pumped his arms, and holding his breath he felt the bat make contact.

The ball soared through the air like a beautiful, white meteor. The boy cried in victory, "Yes!"

Next there was a deafening smash as it shattered the living room window and glass fell everywhere. His mother screamed from somewhere inside the house.

The boy's hands fell limp, letting the bat tumble onto the grass. Across the yard, Tom was laughing.

"You're gonna be in so much shit!"

And he was.

On the pavement, the boy noticed that he was smiling faintly. It had been a long time since he'd smiled. It was comforting, like warm milk inside his new chipped and gap-filled mouth. Two of his teeth had been knocked out in the crash. The boy stuck his tongue into one of the holes, like he used to when he was small and lost them naturally.

The gaps could have been fixed, but the boy had begged his mother not to call the dentist. He didn't want to explain how he'd lost the teeth. He didn't want to have to say that his brother had died, when the dentist asked if everyone in the accident had been OK.

The boy's body was heavy beneath the weight of his soaked clothes. His smile faded, and he felt suddenly very alone. For the first time he felt like Tom wasn't coming back. No more ice cream, no more baseball. No more birthdays (isn't it strange? How people just stop growing one day?).

The emptiness in their house had been shouting at him for the last 3 months and 9 days, but he had refused to listen to the silence. The boy looked down once more at the glass on the road. It was evidence that he could not deny, not only of his brother's existence, but also of his unrelenting absence.

The cold air ran its fingers all over the boy's skin, and he shivered. He considered picking his bike up and going home, crawling into his bed sheets. All he could think about now was how much he would really like to go to sleep.

There was a flash; something had changed. What was it?

The glass on the pavement twinkled. It was ugly, terrible.

The boy looked up.

Green.

KIDS: IF YOU CAN'T BEAT 'EM, LAUGH AT 'EM

DAVE EDWARDS

My name is Eddie Whelehan and I am the father of Calvin from *Calvin and Hobbes*. You know, metaphorically. I mean, I'm not Bill Watterson, I'm just a guy who decided to start recording some of the ridiculous and the sublime things my son says that brings me to my knees. Not metaphorically; I often have to take a knee from laughing at what he says.

My 10 year old son George has always felt older than his years. The way he has always turned a phrase and the way he had girl problems at age 6 meant that he was destined to say and do things that did not coincide with his size/age and destined to provide our family with some solid low-cost entertainment.

This was the one where my wife and I realized that we should maybe start recording some of this gold. It was right after George received a serious talk about the fact that he lied while denying that he had done something wrong:

Age 4 - "I'm not the kind of guy who tells the truth all the time"

And from that moment on, we have done our best to try to get to the green journal as soon as George leaves the room after saying something that makes us shake our heads. I hope you get even a fraction of the joy we have gotten from our son.

Age 5 – Watching TV with Granny, George sees Batman and Robin both caught in a death-trap and says to the screen: "I hope one of you guys has a plan"

Age 5 - Dad: (seeing George is upset on the couch) Do you want some hugs and cuddles?
George: Don't bother – I have no love left in my body.

Age 6, first month of Grade 1 – George has asked mom to come to show and tell with him, and says "but can you put on some lipstick and try to look pretty?"

Age 6 - Talking about a girl in his Grade 1 class: "I'm in L.O.V.E. with her"
  And later on that week George drops this one on us:
  "She has my endless love"

Later on, still at **age 6**, upon meeting another 6 year old girl that has moved in down the street from us:
  "I've got a bad feeling about this girl"
  And
  "I hope she doesn't freak out when I tell her I'm marrying Savannah"

Age 6 - November – Mom and George are playing hairdresser and George says: "Here, let me brush your hair a bit, put in some ponytails – make it a little less messy"

Age 6 - "George, are you still going to be a Jedi when you grow up?"
  "No mom, I'm going to live in a hut down by the lake and build myself fires and stuff"

Age 6 - "The Blackhawks fill me so full of rage"

Age 6, while driving to Marble Slab on a Saturday evening, George made up the following song:
  "Goin' to the store on a Saturday night,
  The flames are getting higher and the birds are taking flight"

Age 6 – George says that he's bored (a common refrain), and when mom suggests that he read a book on the couch he responds with: "Mom, you know I'm the type for action, not relaxin'"

Age 6 – While at work in the morning I noticed that George had put a note in my bag that read "Dad is a butt". When I got home that day mentioned to George how devastated I was to find out that I was a butt and suggested that he should change what he said I was. The next morning when I got to work I found the same note with one alteration. It read: "Dad is a butt ball sack"

Age 7 - July 14 at 10:30pm
Mom and Dad are trying to watch TV downstairs, George is at the top of the stairs to the basement, trying to think of excuses as to why he is still up this late.
"I can't sleep because I'm so hungry…my stomach's as empty as this house before we moved into it."

Age 7 - July 26 - After a *long* fight about staying in his room at night and going to bed
Dad: (frustrated tone) "okay, I'll get you some water so you can stay in your room, is there anything else that you need?"
George: "How about some respect? I don't seem to have any of that.

Age 7 - Aug 16 - I walk into George's bedroom to find him lying face down on his bed in his underwear (backwards of course), which are pulled down below his little bottom:
"My toots are too spicy for my bum"

Age 7 - Sept 16 - Talking about 2 LEGO pieces that don't fit together
"These two pieces don't like each other, like cheese and shredded cheese"

Age 7 - Sept 24 - After calmly but sternly being asked to go to bed nicely because he's way past bedtime and it's Mom's birthday, George says to me:
"Are you about done talking, smart guy?"

Age 7 - Dec 13 - George: "Red Alert, Red Alert – Dad, you need to come to a top secret meeting with me right now.
So I enter his room and we sit on his bed where he puts the blankets over us to talk in secret.
George: (totally serious) "Dad, this is important – Amber said she has a boy in her preschool class that is funnier than me. We can't have this."

I look concerned, but say nothing.
George: "So – what are we going to do about this?"

Age 7 - "Mom, I don't want a lot of peanut butter on my toast, maybe just a light brush of peanut butter today."

Age 8 - Sept 4 – 1st day of School
George has ridden his brand new bike he got in the summer to school for the first time and is going to lock his bike up with his new U-lock. He leaves 20 minutes before Mom drives Indy to school. When Mom and Indy arrive, little George is still standing at the bike racks.
George: "Hey Mom. Can I get a hand over here?"
Mom walks over to the bike rack to find that George has locked both his bike and himself to the bike rack (the lock has gone through the hole in his sleeve). He has been trying to free himself for 15 minutes to get to his first day of school. Mom releases him and he just rolls along – in fact he had already forgotten about it by the time school had ended, noting that nothing of interest had happened on his first day.

Age 8 - Sept 16 - George: Gwillam is so lucky – he's spoiled.
Dad: Well, you're spoiled too, but in a different way. You're spoiled to have a mom, dad and sister that love you more than anything in the whole world.
George: Yeah, well Gwillam's kind of spoiled gets him stuff.

Age 8 - Oct 4 - "Dad I have something I need to tell you. But I can't."
(15 minutes later)
"Dad, I really need to tell you something but I don't want to. Okay, I'll tell you. Wait. I can't."
(8 minutes later)
"Alright, fine. Okay, here it goes: I'minlovewithagirlinmyclassbutIdon'twanttotalkaboutitanymore." (runs out the door into the backyard)

Age 8 - Oct 6 - Mom: "Hey George, how was your day?"
"Scored myself a girlfriend"

Age 8 - Oct 12 - George: Whenever we play Star Wars on the Wii, Gwillam just keeps laughing and Force blasting me when I'm on the ground so I can't get up. It's very disturbing.

Age 8 – December 5 - We were about to play ninjas downstairs and we were creating our characters when George said: "I'm a ninja that has a sword for an arm and can shoot fire out of his other hand."

I responded by saying: "Seriously? C'mon, I've never heard of a ninja that has a sword for an arm and can shoot fire."

George: "Yeah, well now you know one."

Age 9 – March 8 - After throwing up all over our house (including down the back and sides of our couch that was promptly garbaged), I told George that the next he vomited somewhere that wasn't the toilet or a bowl that I would rub his nose in it.

Fast forward to his next fever – we're in bed and we hear his tell-tale 'BLARRR' sound. I go into his room ready to clean up puke off the floor, but his room is empty. George is in the kitchen; he has made his way to the drawer that holds all our bowls/pots, opened it, and thrown up in it. When I get out there, he lifts up his head, looks at me and musters up enough strength to hoarsely whisper: "Ta-Da"

Age 9 - July 16 - George is learning how to pitch for the first time. After teaching him the basics of the two different windups, George takes the ball onto the pretend mound and, dismissing everything he was just told, spends the rest of our time together trying to figure out what his "signature move" is going to be as a pitcher. (He finally goes with resting his knee, leg and throwing fist on the ground, Thor-style after each pitch)

Age 10 - Oct 28: George had his French Test ripped up because his teacher accused him of cheating. He had the answers written up his arm. But he explained to me that he was just doing that to study *before* his test. I was tempted to believe that he actually was not cheating (because that's exactly the kind of thing someone who doesn't think like anyone else would think is a normal way to study) until he informed me that he was also caught having taped the answers to the bottom of his desk. I think he may have cheated.

So we'll continue to try to record the moments that make us smile (usually in hindsight) and we'll continue to get as much enjoyment as we can out of all of the hilarious/brilliant/frustrating things that come with parenting our little guy. He truly does make things more interesting.
    And it looks like we'll have to get another colour of journal.

George's youger sister Moopsie just turned 7 and also has the family talent for phrasing and melodrama.

Moopsie - **Age 6**: "Going to school is a big waste of clean panties"

41834632R00068

Made in the USA
Charleston, SC
12 May 2015